THE BELL REEF

THE BELL REEF

Sarita Kendall

Illustrated by
Mark Hudson

Houghton Mifflin Company
Boston 1990

Library of Congress Cataloging-in-Publication Data

Kendall, Sarita.
  The bell reef / Sarita Kendall ; illustrated by Mark Hudson.
    p. cm.
  Summary: Anxious to recover the sunken treasure of a famous pirate
ship, two teenagers enlist the help of a trained dolphin and
determine to carry out their hunt despite the ghost stories and
mysterious underwater noises surrounding the Reef.
  ISBN 0-395-53354-6
  [1. Buried treasure—Fiction. 2. Adventure and adventurers—
Fiction.] I. Hudson, Mark, 1961–   ill. II. Title.
PZ7.K35Be   1990   89-24708
[Fic]—dc20   CIP
                        AC

First American edition 1990
Originally published in Great Britain in 1989 by Macmillan Publishers Ltd.

Printed in the United States of America

FFG 10 9 8 7 6 5 4 3 2 1

Contents

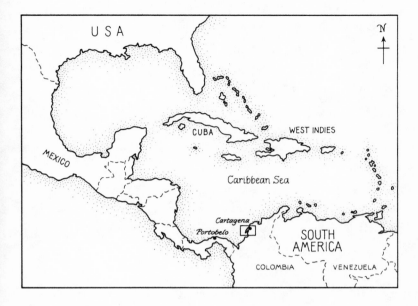

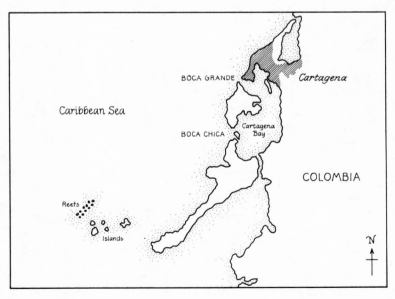

1 Friday: the island

As he paddled his canoe round the point, Daniel saw one of the dolphins leap clear of the water. Kika! he thought, and rested the paddle on his knees, watching. She burst up again in a shower of spray, and seemed to stop, poised in mid-air, for a moment. Then the dark grey back arched over until her head almost touched her tail, and she plummeted down, breaking the surface with barely a splash.

From the bobbing canoe, Daniel could see she was jumping far higher than the fence which separated the dolphin pen from the open sea. He wondered why she didn't choose freedom if she could clear the fence so easily.

A wave slopped over the stern and Daniel remembered he was already later than usual. The strong wind and choppy sea had slowed him down this morning: the dolphins must be hungry. Once across the coral reef which jutted out from the island, the water changed colour from deep blue to light green. He paddled hard, aiming for the sheltered inlet near the aquarium. The afternoon before he had left a large block of fish to defrost in the

1

cooler – with luck there would be enough to satisfy the three dolphins.

Sliding the canoe in by a stone step, Daniel hopped out and tied up to a post – the small island was surrounded by rocky coral, and there were no proper beaches. On still, sunny days it was sweltering; but Daniel preferred that to the hot, gritty wind which always made everyone snappy.

Pedro, the island boatman, was sitting on the step, winding fishing-line on to a piece of wood.

'Why didn't you come out last night? You should see the snapper I caught!' His Spanish had the swinging accent of the Caribbean. 'Are you too busy with the dolphins to go fishing nowadays?'

'Of course not . . . but I must run, I'm late already.' Daniel loped off towards the aquarium. He ran by the kitchen, and on past the small fish pens inside the aquarium entrance. The tide was out and the water level looked low, but the pens were not crowded enough to endanger the fish. Next came deeper enclosures holding sharks, jewfish, rays and turtles, and, last of all, the dolphins. Their pen took up more space than the rest of the aquarium; the end faced the open sea, and there was a long wooden pier along one side.

Kika popped up, snout and flippers above

2

the water, to greet Daniel. The long line of her mouth curved round either side of her head, almost as far as her eyes. Forgetting it was against training rules, he waved at her. Kika reacted immediately, rolling over on to one side, her pale pink belly half out of the water. She splashed enthusiastically with a supple grey flipper, imitating his wave. Daniel looked round guiltily, but no one else had come out to the aquarium yet. Kika so obviously enjoyed showing off – it seemed unfairly strict to limit her fun to short training sessions.

The cooler was at the far end of the pier, and Kika was already peeking up at it by the time Daniel got there. She opened her mouth wide, showing an impressive set of sharp white teeth and a rosy, curling tongue. The fish smelled fine. Daniel checked each one before slicing its head off, and the dolphins' yellow plastic buckets filled quickly. Choosing three of the biggest fish, he cut them open to stuff in some vitamin pills. Just as he was finishing Jane came hurriedly down the pier. She was wearing a blue patterned skirt and white top instead of her bathing suit, which puzzled Daniel for a moment.

'Everything ready?' she asked, and Daniel nodded. 'Well, you go ahead and feed them – I won't be doing any training today. I have to go into Cartagena to the dentist. It's Vicky's half-term and she has a week off school, so she'll be coming back with me.'

Daniel wasn't sure he had understood perfectly (Jane's Spanish was dreadful) but he caught the general idea. He was pleased to have the dolphins to himself; on the other hand, it was going to be a bore having Vicky around for a few days. She was a year younger than Daniel and behaved as though she was the world's greatest dolphin expert – unlike her mother, who really did know dolphins, but never made him feel stupid. Jane was so friendly and active: even her walk, going back up the pier, was springy, with her brown pony-tail bouncing from side to side. Everyone on the island liked her, though they didn't understand half of what she said.

The dolphins were swimming up and down impatiently, confused by Jane's departure. Daniel put the buckets of fish on to a float, and jumped on neatly, pushing off just hard enough to land up alongside the wooden platform anchored in the middle of the dolphin pen. Kika was by far the quickest and greediest, so he began to throw her fish out on one side while he hand-fed Molly and Pacho on the other.

Jane insisted they weren't ready to put on a show yet, though Kika was learning very fast. It was only six months since the dolphins had been captured by local fishermen and brought

4

to the aquarium. At first all three had looked alike to Daniel, with slate-grey backs and heads, fading to pinkish white underneath. Now he knew the way each one jumped, swam and breathed, as well as the nick out of Molly's tail, the ragged dorsal fin on Pacho's back, and Kika's noisy squeaks.

Daniel leaned out to give Pacho the last mouthful, avoiding Kika's interfering snout. He almost toppled over and, grabbing at the platform to steady himself, knocked the trainer's whistle into the sea. Daniel panicked for a moment and jumped in after it, but he soon realised he'd have to go back to the pier for a mask. The wind had churned up the sea and sand, making the water much murkier than usual.

With the mask on he dived and swam round and round, inspecting every rock and shadow. Kika hovered close by, watching him. After several tries he still couldn't find the whistle. Where could it have gone? Anxious, Daniel pushed the mask up on his forehead and rested, holding on to the platform. It had to happen today, with Jane in Cartagena; she would think him so careless, just a dumb island boy who couldn't be trusted to do things right on his own. And only yesterday she'd congratulated him for organising the dolphins' feeding so efficiently.

Well, he'd have to look again, and again, until he found it. As Daniel let go of the platform to pull his mask down, he heard a metallic clink; there was a small splash, and he realised something must have fallen in. Now what had happened? Everything seemed to be going wrong. He ducked, and peered down in time to see a silvery object spinning towards the bottom. The whistle! It was impossible . . . what on earth was going on . . . how could it have been back on the platform? The whistle disappeared in the cloudy sea. Suddenly, Daniel felt water swirling round his legs, and Kika shot past underneath him. She went straight for the bottom, then torpedoed up beside him, holding something in her mouth.

Daniel could hardly believe it – she'd got the whistle. Oh no, he thought, now she'll swallow it and I'll really be in trouble. But Kika flicked her head, and the whistle tinkled on the platform. So that was it! She'd taught herself a new trick without any help from Jane. Kika seemed just as delighted with her cleverness as Daniel was. She jumped twice, chirped, and went off to join Pacho and Molly.

Would she fetch it again? Daniel was tempted to try, but he decided not to risk it: Jane had once said she could tell immediately if anyone else worked with the dolphins.

In spite of the wind, the day was muggy and

banks of dark, billowing clouds were building up. Sometimes the waves were too strong for Daniel to paddle back to the island where he lived with his mother, grandfather and sisters. His father was rarely at home: he worked on the big tourist boat which brought people out from Cartagena to marvel at the beauties of the islands.

Daniel had left school a year before when he got the job at the aquarium. He'd hung around at weekends, making himself useful in the hope that Antonio Silva, the owner, would notice. It had worked, and he'd been offered a small wage. Daniel looked older than he really was: dark-skinned and lanky, with curly black hair, he was a typical islander in every way except one – he had a dreamer's grey-green eyes. There must have been black slaves, European sailors and Caribbean Indians among his ancestors.

His great ambition was to have a power boat, and to swish past small canoes like his own, leaving them awash in his wake.

The dolphins were enjoying the rough weather. Kika rode a long wave into the far corner of the pen, and went streaking back to the outer fence to pick up another. She must have had much more fun when the whole ocean was her playground, thought Daniel. He went in past the sharks and the cumbersome, heavy-breathing turtles to fetch another block of frozen fish from the storehouse.

Tourists were so fascinated by the sharks that they often climbed down on to the shark feeding platform to take photographs – luckily there had been no clumsy slips.

But (apart from the dolphins, of course) Daniel liked the small, brilliantly coloured reef fish best. Striped, splodged and delicately painted in every shade of red, green, orange, purple and blue, they darted in and out among the rocks and conch shells.

The tourist boat was due to arrive at any moment, and the tables in the thatched open-air restaurant were being laid for lunch. Daniel sneaked into the kitchen to beg a snack; he didn't get lunch until everyone had been taken round the aquarium and the dolphins had been fed again. The kitchen was stifling. Fat sizzled in huge pans, the cook looked hot and cross, and Daniel escaped quickly with a raisin cake.

During feeding he heard a high-powered launch approaching; then a red bow appeared, cutting through a cloud of spray; the boat circled the reef and disappeared behind some squat green mangroves, heading for the dock.

If it hadn't been for the big chart spread out on a table in the corner of the restaurant, Daniel wouldn't have given the red boat

9

another thought. But when he went in to eat lunch, three men were hunched over the chart, arguing loudly in English. So they were gringos – foreigners, probably Americans – he thought.

Daniel got a quick look at the chart as he passed the table; part of it seemed to be covered with circles and symbols, marked on in red. Maps didn't mean much to Daniel – he could recognise Colombia's shape and that was about all – so he wasn't very interested until he heard the words 'San José galleon'. Even with his scanty English he could understand that. People had been searching for the *San José* galleon as long as he could remember. It had been sunk near the islands centuries ago, with a fabulous treasure on board.

As he ate his fried fish and rice, Daniel strained to hear what the men were saying. It was already nearly three o'clock and there was nobody else around. They probably thought Daniel couldn't understand them, and didn't bother to keep their voices down. From the little he could follow, Daniel knew they were discussing diving and diving equipment. Words like 'compressors', 'air tanks' and 'regulator', which were similar in Spanish, kept cropping up.

Well, that made sense. If they were interested

in the *San José* they would have to dive for it, because the Spanish galleon was supposed to lie in deep water off some shoals called the Treasure Banks. There were so many wrecks in the sea around Cartagena that divers often found ancient cannon or coral-crusted silver coins. But the *San José* was in a class on its own, and small fortunes had been spent on electronic gadgetry in the hope of discovering its treasure.

Daniel was drifting into a daydream of a shadowy ship's keel half buried in glinting gold when he saw the men stubbing out cigarettes and getting up to go.

'We came to see Antonio Silva. Do you know when he'll be back?' asked a big, bearded man, speaking reasonable Spanish.

'He took somebody in to Cartagena,' said Daniel. 'If the wind doesn't get any stronger they'll be back later.'

'We can't wait around, it's already pretty rough out there for our boat. Will you be sure to tell Antonio that Ray Macdonald came to see him? Just a minute, maybe I've got a business card.' He picked a card out of his wallet and handed it to Daniel. 'Give him that. We'll drop by another day.'

Daniel was longing to ask whether they had found the *San José*, but he didn't want to admit he'd been eavesdropping. The card

11

had the name of an American company on it: UNITED OIL – DEEP SEA SERVICES. He left it in the storeroom, thinking he'd have a chance to find out more when he gave it to Antonio.

2 Friday: Cartagena

Antonio Silva wove his way in among the launches and fishing boats, and edged along-side the harbour quay. Jane jumped off, and they agreed to meet later at the marina where Antonio left the boat. The quay was packed with people: families loading bulky sacks into canoes, women roasting bananas over char-coal grills, and boys shouting 'To Barú! To Bocachica! Take your place now!'

Jane walked through the archway to the Spanish colonial part of Cartagena, passing under the clock tower and the massive stone walls which surrounded the old city.

The flat they had rented was on the third floor of a tall corner house. It had a wooden balcony looking over the battlements to the open sea, and there was nearly always a breeze to keep the flat cool. Vicky and her father lived there during the week, going out to the island for weekends. Jane sometimes felt guilty about leaving them on their own, but she hadn't been able to resist the dolphin training job.

It had all happened so quickly: they'd gone one Sunday in the tourist boat to visit the

13

islands; Jane had trained seals and dolphins at a zoo, and when she heard there were dolphins on one of the islands, she just had to see them. She'd asked Antonio whether he was planning to put on a show. They'd talked for hours about the idea, and he'd said she was just the person he needed: would she take over the training? Vicky and her father were a bit glum about it at first, but they liked the thought of spending the weekends snorkelling round coral reefs on a Caribbean island.

Jane had asked Rosa, a solid, friendly woman who lived on the ground floor, whether she knew anyone who could help with the housework and keep an eye on Vicky after school. Rosa herself was pleased to earn some extra money. Her husband was a shoemaker, and they were saving for a motor scooter to speed up deliveries. Rosa much preferred being at home to cutting and shaping leather in the stuffy workshop. She adored Vicky and spoiled her terribly, much to Jane's annoyance. Vicky often spent her afternoons downstairs with Rosa's family, and as a result her Spanish had become very good.

'Oof, it's awfully hot and thundery in the city,' said Jane as Rosa let her into the flat. 'How's everyone? Any problems this week?'

'We're all fine. Vicky asked me to tell

14

you school stops at midday today. And your husband wants you to call him.'

Jane had the impression that Rosa disapproved of her casual approach to family life. She dialled her husband's office at the oil refinery.

'Martin, can we all meet for lunch? Vicky will be out by then, and I'll need something to strengthen me for the dentist.'

'Well, there's a snarl-up with the new terminal, and I'm going to have to go over there this afternoon. We'll be busy all weekend, so I don't think I'll make it to the island. Tell you what, if you have time to come out here, we could at least have a canteen lunch together.'

It was easy to pick Vicky out by the school entrance. She was the tallest in her group, a tanned, skinny beanpole with short fairish hair and brown eyes. What a nuisance, thought Jane, she's growing out of her uniform already, and her fringe needs trimming. Vicky came bounding over.

'Lots of homework?' asked Jane.

'Not too bad. We're supposed to write a story about pirates in Cartagena, and some geometry.'

'We must get a bus, we're going to the refinery for lunch,' said Jane.

Once clear of the old narrow streets the

15

bus roared along the highway behind Cartagena Bay towards the industrial zone. Factories lined the road, and spilled their waste into the bay, poisoning its waters. Outside one of them there was a long queue of trucks, and the drivers were lounging in hammocks slung between the wheels.

A security guard gave Jane and Vicky passes for the refinery offices. In the distance they could see a maze of gleaming yellow- and silver-painted pipes, tanks and funnels. Martin had been sent to Cartagena for two years by his company to help build an extension to the refinery. As usual, he was scarlet with rage about the bureaucracy, about everyone's inefficiency and about delays to his project. The air-conditioning wasn't working, and strands of thin fair hair stuck to his forehead.

'We've got a firm laying the underwater pipe for the oil terminal, and some of the divers seem to be taking holidays before they're due. Our time-table just doesn't allow for that.' He sighed, and rubbed his brown eyes tiredly.

Vicky enjoyed going to her father's office: his Colombian colleagues always made a fuss of her and admired her Spanish. The canteen food wasn't bad, she thought as she tucked into a coconut ice-cream buried in chocolate sauce – enough to make a dentist shudder.

'Keep away from the sharks,' joked Martin as he kissed them goodbye. 'And tell Daniel I haven't forgotten about the waterproof torch he asked me for.'

'I don't know why Dad bothers with that torch,' said Vicky crossly as they went back to the city. 'Daniel's just trying it on.'

'You're being unfair. Daniel's earned it, taking us for boat-rides in his spare time. Why are you so anti him?' Jane knew Vicky and Daniel didn't get on, and assumed there must be some jealousy over the dolphins.

'He's so boring. He can only think about fishing and boats. Of course, he thinks you're wonderful.' Vicky shrugged and turned her face away to stop further questions.

Antonio, dark and wiry in his blue bathing trunks, was already waiting by the time they'd escaped the dentist and got to the marina. He was anxious to leave quickly because of the storm clouds. Vicky changed into a red bathing suit and stowed her clothes and canvas bag under the tarpaulin in the bow. They whizzed across the sheltered bay, spray flying off the tops of the waves and drenching everything. The big tourist boat was on its way back, passengers clustered on the stern deck to escape being soaked. It must be really rough outside the bay, thought Vicky, worried.

Strong gusts of wind and rain buffeted the boat as they headed for Bocachica, the opening of the bay. On either side of Bocachica (meaning Little Mouth in Spanish) stood a stately stone fortress, once armed with heavy cannon batteries. The other entrance to the bay at Bocagrande (Big Mouth) had long been blocked by sunken hulks and an underwater wall to stop pirates and enemy warships from sailing through. Cartagena was one of South America's great ports in colonial days, and the Spanish treasure fleets that anchored in the bay needed protection.

Lightning zigzagged down to the water, and a sharp crackle of thunder startled Vicky. It was difficult to tell which was worse by now, the rain or the spray.

The boat slammed into the troughs between the huge waves, jarring so badly that Antonio had to slow right down. His cap jammed firmly over his ears, he stood easily at the wheel while Vicky and her mother clutched for handholds to steady themselves against the rolling and pitching. If they hadn't had such confidence in Antonio's seamanship, the heavy sea would have been terrifying.

Vicky watched the seesawing horizon anxiously, and cheered up as soon as a grey blob of land appeared ahead. A

18

mass of birds – pelicans, boobies and frigate birds – swooped and hovered above the tiny islet near the main island. The row they made was tremendous. No one disturbed them here, and there must have been hundreds of nests in the dozen windswept trees that clung to the broken coral.

After dumping her bag in the cabin Jane used, Vicky ran off to the aquarium. Normally she would have dived straight in to join the dolphins, but the crossing had left her feeling cold and shaky. She sat on the edge of the pier swinging her legs while Kika swam around below, surfacing frequently in her 'look-out' position to check on Vicky. It was hard not to imagine that Kika was smiling with pleasure – only Vicky was too accustomed to dolphins to make that mistake. Jane was always reminding her that dolphins could be very intelligent without having the same feelings as humans.

Kika darted around underwater, chasing something. Suddenly a big brown and white spotted sting-ray broke the surface and flipped over the wave crests. Kika leaped up behind, landing almost on top of it as she re-entered the water.

Vicky knew that rays didn't sting if they were left alone but this one might well react to being tossed around. The strong barb in its tail could give Kika a painful wound. She went in to look for someone to catch the ray and transfer it to another pen.

Daniel had given Ray Macdonald's card to Antonio and was waiting to see whether he would make any comment.

'Didn't he say what it was about?' asked Antonio.

'No,' said Daniel, 'though I think it might be something to do with the *San José*. They had a big chart.'

'Aha, more treasure hunters. It's funny, I know the name but I can't remember where from. What does he look like?'

'He's big and heavy with a gingery beard. The others were all gringos too.'

Antonio passed the card to Jane. 'Your husband's in the oil business – does the name mean anything to you?'

'Why, yes. Not the person, but the company. I think United Oil is doing the pipe-laying for the oil terminal. Martin said he was fed up with the divers for playing truant.'

'That's it! Ray Macdonald's a professional diver. I've met him once, and I've heard a lot of gossip about him.'

At that moment Vicky found them and explained the sting-ray problem. Antonio went straight out to the dolphins' pen with her. Annoyed that the conversation had been cut short, Daniel untied his canoe and paddled off home. As he neared his island, he noticed that the coral rubble and sand on the exposed side of the spit had been shifted far to the south by the storm.

3 Saturday: the reef

Vicky was woken by Antonio's parrots. They seemed to be having a squawking competition in a tree just outside the window. 'Tonio! Tonio!' shrieked one, and the other answered with exaggerated laughter. Vicky lay in bed for a moment enjoying the idea that she had a whole week on the island, then bounced up noisily.

'Come on, Mum, it must be nearly time for the first training session. Look, it's a fantastic day; the water will be so clear!'

'Mmmm. I'm on my way, but coffee comes first. How about getting me a cup from the kitchen?'

Vicky made a face. 'You can get it on your way to the aquarium. I'm off.'

Barefooted, she jogged along the path through the mangroves and took a short-cut to the dolphin pen by climbing over the fence round the aquarium.

Daniel was in the water, wearing his mask.

'Hey, you know my mother doesn't like anyone to swim with the dolphins just before training,' shouted Vicky.

'The knife fell in,' said Daniel shortly, hauling himself out on to the pier. He set to work preparing the fish.

The sea was extraordinarily calm, and Vicky could see every twist and twirl of the dolphins underwater. Kika, of course, was the most active. She was annoying a porcupine fish, which defended itself by gulping sea-water and air so it swelled up into a ball three times its normal size. Kika was careful not to go within range of the sharp spines which stuck out all over the bloated body.

Jane and Antonio came out sipping their coffee and discussing plans for the dolphin show.

'If we go on show too soon, it'll be a solo act. Kika's so far ahead of the others. Maybe Pacho's a bit dumb. Molly could learn quicker, I'm sure, but she's under Pacho's thumb – mmm – I mean flipper.'

Kika's training went very well. She jumped higher than ever, sometimes as much as ten feet clear of the rope which Daniel held above the water. Pacho made everyone laugh with a series of splashy belly-flops; Molly stayed in the background, only coming up to the platform to take her fish from Daniel's hand.

'The water's rarely as perfect as this,' said Antonio as they were all eating breakfast. 'Why don't you go snorkelling on one of the ocean reefs? There's more than three hours before the next session.'

'Yes. Yes! Let's, Mum,' burbled Vicky.

It was agreed that Daniel would take Vicky and Jane out towards the Treasure Banks. Antonio suggested they try the Bell Reef, which would be about twenty feet below the surface at low tide.

'Any sharks?' asked Vicky.

'Only little ones,' teased Antonio. 'Don't worry, they wouldn't bother you. But look out for ghosts; I've heard people say it's a haunted reef.'

Vicky, who was less scared of ghosts than of sharks, rushed off enthusiastically to collect the gear.

The launch skimmed over the blue-green shallows to the darker open sea. Daniel speeded up so fiercely that they could barely squint ahead, their eyes smarting in the wind and sun. He seemed quite different driving the boat, thought Vicky, excitable, and pleased to be in charge.

Fifteen minutes out they passed the last of the islands, a long low shape with tall palms growing behind a beautiful beach. It was government-owned and uninhabited, but boat-loads of trespassers occasionally picnicked on shore. Another ten minutes and the sea suddenly changed to a pale aquamarine colour.

24

Daniel slowed, and stopped the engine. 'From what Antonio said, this must be the Bell Reef.'

The boat rose and fell in a slight swell, drifting with the current. They could see dark rocky outlines and sandy patches underneath.

'We'll throw the painter out. Keep a hand on the rope all the time so we don't get separated from the boat,' said Jane.

With masks and flippers tightly strapped on, they plunged into the sea. Daniel took the end of the rope and swam until it was stretched to its full fifty feet, while the others spread out between him and the boat. Vicky looked down: it was a moment before the reef shifted into focus. Suddenly she saw a field of plum-coloured fan-like corals waving gently just under her. The tips seemed so close she thought she must be able to touch them, but she soon realised they were far below. The sea was already a bit rougher, and now and then water splashed into her snorkel.

A large school of silvery jacks with yellow tails moved swiftly along the edge of the reef, looking for food. Daniel dived down to take a closer look at a small green moray eel, which was waving its head around outside a cleft in the rock. Vertically-striped sergeant majors and horizontally striped grunts threaded their way through the reef. Blue-green parrot-fish with

red and yellow markings ate seaweed cemented to the rock, their sharp teeth grinding the coral into sand.

With so much activity, it was easy to miss the hermit crab furiously waving its claws, defending its shell against an enemy; or the long, thin trumpet-fish lurking upright among some branches of coral, ready to grab a shrimp that swam too close; or even the well-camouflaged and thoroughly poisonous scorpion-fish, almost invisible against grey-brown rock. In some parts of the islands the coral was dying because polluted water from the mainland rivers reached far out into the ocean. The Bell Reef was clearly very much alive, though the tiny coral-building creatures were too small to be seen by the snorkellers.

Jane tugged the rope and pointed to the left: a three-foot barracuda was hovering above the reef, watching them, but keeping well away. They moved along the reef bit by bit, following the drift of the boat. Vicky couldn't see any likeness to a bell shape, and wondered about the name. It was a little eerie looking down at another world out in the middle of the ocean, she thought. Daniel was concerned with more practical matters – such as going back to the reef some other time with a net and a bucket to try to catch fish for the aquarium.

'I've had enough,' called Jane. 'But you

stay a bit longer if you want.' She swam back to the boat and slopped sunscreen lotion on, then settled uncomfortably on the floorboards.

They were on the end of the reef now, and could see how sharply it shelved down to a deep sandy bottom. Daniel dived but he couldn't hold his breath long enough to explore the branches of elkhorn coral sticking out along the edge of the reef. He was shooting back to the surface through the sun-dappled water when a sudden gleam from the bottom surprised him. It was as if a mirror had reflected the sun. A few deep breaths, and he swam down again. Although he stayed down until he was dizzy, he couldn't see anything which could have produced that strange gleam.

Vicky watched curiously: she was sure Daniel was looking for something specific, not just enjoying the underwater scenery. He seemed to be staying down such a long time. As he came up she thought she saw something twinkle at the edge of the coral. Maybe that had caught his eye; and though she couldn't go as deep as he did, she swam down to investigate. She concentrated on the ocean floor. It was much colder at this depth.

Suddenly, a violent clanging jolted her so fiercely she felt as if she'd been struck. She gasped and swallowed a mouthful of sea-water.

The deafening noise went on booming weirdly through the water. Terrified, Vicky kicked desperately for the surface. Coughing and spluttering, she asked 'What was that?' as soon as she could speak.

'It's me knocking on the side of the boat,' shouted Jane. 'If you'd been holding on to the rope as I told you to, you would have realised I was trying to call you. It's time to go.'

Vicky looked round at Daniel. He was still wearing his mask and snorkel, and she couldn't see his expression.

'I'm sure it wasn't that, Mum. Do it again.'

Jane gave the hull a few more knocks and Vicky put her head under. No, there was nothing frightening about that, it was a completely different sound. The clanging had throbbed right through her, making her head ring and her fingers tingle. It had been so close; what was it, where could it have come from? Of course, how stupid I am, this is the Bell Reef; there must be a bell here, thought Vicky.

'Come on you two.' Jane sounded impatient, and she didn't understand the delay.

As they climbed back into the boat Vicky asked Daniel if he'd heard anything strange. He shook his head, and got busy starting the engine.

'Antonio's talk about ghosts seems to have got to you,' laughed Jane, giving Vicky a hug.

29

Daniel revved the motor, and they headed back to the island. Vicky wondered whether the others hadn't heard the clanging because their heads had been above the water. But it had been so loud ... She was distracted by two graceful silvery-blue flying fish; they glided along beside the boat for over a hundred yards, their huge front fins spread out like wings.

After a hot training session and the standard fried fish lunch, Jane announced she was going to read in the cabin. Vicky, always happier in the water than out of it on a baking day, went back to the dolphin pen. She kept her tee-shirt on over her bathing suit to protect her shoulders from the sun, and floated around watching the dolphins.

Pacho and Molly repeated the same pattern over and over again: they surfaced for a breath, briefly opening the blowholes on the tops of their heads, then dived to the bottom and swam towards the platform. Vicky had counted about forty-five seconds between each breath, though the dolphins sometimes stayed under much longer.

Kika swam all over the pen, and Vicky could never guess where she would pop up. She was chasing a leaf along the fence, catching it in her mouth and then letting go so it drifted in the water. Vicky darted in to pick it up, and swam off with it. She turned quickly when Kika appeared in front of her, but she couldn't match Kika's speed or skill, and gave the leaf back. Though it was a one-sided game of catch, Kika was obviously enjoying the attention, and kept releasing the leaf where Vicky could collect it.

When they were both bored with the leaf game, Vicky looked around for some other entertainment. She caught one end of the rope Jane used for training Kika to jump (the other end was tied to the pier fence-post) and pulled it with her as she dived to the bottom. Kika raced past to snatch a trailing loop. Between them, they invented enough rope games to exhaust them.

Kika bobbed at the surface, gently nudging Vicky and enjoying being stroked. She turned in the water, offering the firm, grainy skin of her flanks to be rubbed. Being with the dolphins had washed away the uneasiness that Vicky had felt ever since she heard the clanging on the reef. She scrambled out, coiled the rope carefully on the pier, and went in. But she didn't realise that the end had fallen through the wooden slats to dangle just above the water.

Daniel was working with Luis, who was responsible for feeding the sharks, the turtles and all the fish in the aquarium. They sat cross-legged, either side of a large wood

31

slab, gutting fish and slicing heads off. Luis chattered and joked without stopping. He was one of the best fishermen in the islands, and a distant cousin of Daniel's. If anyone knew the reefs well, it was Luis, and Daniel decided to ask him about the fishing on the Bell Reef. Luis didn't really answer, and talked about a place where he'd caught snapper, on the other side of the government island.

'Is there something odd about the Bell Reef?' insisted Daniel.

'Too many sharks, too many stories, too much noise for fish,' joked Luis. 'I like quiet places.'

Daniel knew perfectly well that Luis wouldn't be put off by a few sharks, and they hadn't seen any that morning. As for fish, the reef was as crowded as any he'd ever been on. That left the stories and the noise. He hadn't admitted it to Vicky, but he had heard a faint ringing sound, even above the water. She must have heard something much louder for it to have scared her so. He wondered if she'd seen anything too. Perhaps he would ask her the next day, if she wasn't in one of her bossy moods. It was time to go home.

4 Sunday: the rope

Sunday was the busiest day of the week at the aquarium: the tourist boat was packed, and other visitors also stopped by for lunch. Daniel was paddling his way towards the island before seven o'clock when he saw a tremendous splashing in the dolphin pen. He went straight for the pier instead of taking his canoe round to the inlet. One of the dolphins must be in trouble: through the wire-netting and pier supports he could see tail-flukes slapping the water. As soon as he got on to the pier, he realised it was Kika, thrashing desperately to get free: the training rope was wound tightly around her body, and around a column under the pier. She could barely raise her head far enough out of the water to breathe. Molly and Pacho had left their corner, and were swimming agitatedly back and forth underneath Kika, occasionally pushing her upwards for air.

Daniel jumped in and held Kika at the surface while he talked to her and tried to calm her. He couldn't touch the bottom, and she was too frightened to let him unravel the rope. First he should have untied the end attached to the fence-post up above, he thought. Someone in flip-flop sandals came running along overhead, and he shouted: 'Undo the rope, quick.'

It was Vicky. She pulled at the stiff knot, gradually working it loose. Once the end was undone, the rope no longer cut into Kika. She relaxed and Daniel was able to free her. She didn't seem to have been harmed, but Daniel imagined she'd be very wary of the rope in future. He handed it up to Vicky, and got out himself.

Daniel was upset. Kika could so easily have drowned. He was in charge of the training equipment, and if the rope had fallen in, it was his fault for not putting it away properly after the last training session. He knew Jane would be furious and he expected Vicky to take advantage of his mistake. Much to his surprise, she just stood there looking at the rope.

'You know,' she said unhappily, 'I had the rope in the pen yesterday afternoon. I'm sure I left it on top of the pier, out of the water. Somebody else may have moved it afterwards, but . . . '

It was a great relief for Daniel to learn that he wasn't to blame. He was grateful that Vicky should even admit she had used the rope – someone else might easily have kept quiet. 'If you'd rather, we won't tell your mother,' he said.

Vicky shook her head, though she thought it was nice of him: 'She'll know something has happened when she starts Kika jumping – Kika won't want to go near the rope.'

Daniel went to get the fish ready. Vicky followed, and offered to help for the first time ever. Jane, arriving for training, was amazed by the sight of the fair and dark heads working side by side, but swallowed a tactless comment.

'I'm going to try a new approach today,' she told them, gathering her hair up in a slide. 'We won't use the rope at all. Kika has to get used to jumping with my hand signal.'

Daniel understood the 'no rope' bit, but not the rest. Vicky scolded her mother for her bad Spanish and repeated the sentence, adding that it would be interesting to see how Kika reacted. Daniel got the point: they wouldn't tell Jane about the rope incident unless Kika behaved so strangely that they had to.

Jane assumed that Kika's lack of concentration was due to the change in routine, and nothing was said about the rope. Kika jumped through the hoop effortlessly; at the beginning she wouldn't even put her head through it in the water. It had taken a lot of patient work by Jane to persuade her to swim through, let alone jump. The dolphins hated anything enclosing them and refused to enter small spaces until they had complete confidence in their trainer.

After breakfast Vicky hung around the store-room while Daniel was digging out the next block of fish. She wanted to ask him what he'd seen and heard on the reef, but she felt unusually shy, and fidgeted in the doorway kicking her sandal against the step. He's pretty strong, she thought, surprised at the size of the block he lifted from the freezer. He never wore a shirt, and his back and arms were black and shining with sweat.

'You know, I did hear that noise yesterday – as if someone was hammering rivets into a ship's hull,' said Daniel suddenly. 'But it wasn't much, and I thought maybe I'd imagined it until you came rocketing up.'

'It wasn't much! What do you mean?' exclaimed Vicky. 'It was like . . . like breaking the sound barrier or something, a fantastic *boing*.'

'Maybe it sounded louder because you were down there on your own, and didn't expect anything— '

Vicky interrupted. 'I heard it . . . I'm telling you it was incredibly loud. That must be why it's called the Bell Reef. But didn't you see something there? You went down deep, looking.'

'Yes . . . no . . . I'm not sure. I thought I saw this bright glittery light at the edge of the reef.'

'Me too,' said Vicky excitedly, pulling her fingers so sharply they cracked. 'What do you think it could be?'

'I've been wondering; the sun was shining through the water quite strongly. It seemed as though there was a light there, but I guess it would have to be something made of glass or metal.' Daniel didn't tell her that he was hoping there might be a wreck on the sea-bed. He knew that coral could grow over the remains of a ship, hiding it so well that not a piece of metal or timber could be seen – or the keel might be buried deep in the sand.

Vicky was already creating her own fantasies: 'Imagine if a pirate ship sank in a battle, or a Spanish galleon full of gold! That still doesn't explain the noise, though.'

Daniel was half annoyed that she'd immediately thought of a wreck. She'd probably go round telling everyone. 'Why don't we keep quiet about it? I want to go back and have another look. I'd like to try to catch a fish or two for the aquarium.'

'Yes! Could we go today? Everyone's always in such a rush on Sundays. Would Antonio let you take the boat? Shall we ask him?'

Vicky's enthusiasm flummoxed Daniel for a moment. He'd planned to go on his own, or perhaps with one of his island friends. On the other hand, if he took Vicky, Antonio would probably lend him the speed-boat; otherwise he'd have to use his canoe, and that would take for ever.

'Okay, you ask him, he's bound to say yes to you. What about your mother, wouldn't she want to come?'

'I don't think so, she said this morning that she's way behind with her notes on the dolphins' training. I'll go and find Antonio.'

Vicky didn't have to go far. Antonio was leaning against the railing telling a group of visitors about the lemon shark – it was the most dangerous one in the aquarium. Lemon sharks sometimes went into very shallow water along the beaches; many of them had been killed because the Cartagena city authorities thought they would scare tourists away. Luis, who had been standing by, put on a thick glove and stepped down on to the platform to feed the nurse sharks; they thrust their mouths up by his feet to take the fish from him, and the crowd oohed and aahed. Antonio noted their reactions with interest; he put a great deal of effort into the aquarium, and liked to see it being appreciated.

He hesitated before saying no to Vicky; he

was sorry to refuse her, but it was already a bit late, and Daniel would miss the next training session.

'Today's not a good day for it. How about tomorrow, though, if it's fine? I tell you what,' he was watching a group of people in eye-catching shirts and sunhats ambling along the pier towards the dolphins, 'you go and give those people a lesson on dolphins. They're always interested, and most of that lot are North Americans. They'll understand you better than me.' Antonio knew Vicky would enjoy lecturing the small crowd. He stayed in the background to listen while she skipped willingly down the pier.

'What kind of dolphins are they?' asked a woman in a black bikini, her face camouflaged behind silver sunglasses.

'They're called *Sotalia Fluviatilis*,' said Vicky importantly, as though she was making a speech in a school hall. 'Sotalia live in the Amazon rivers, and along the coast of Brazil, and in this part of the Caribbean. You can see they're much smaller than bottle-nose dolphins, which are the ones usually kept in aquariums. Some fishermen found these three in a bay nearby. Pacho – the male, over there – seemed to be sick, but he recovered.' Vicky hesitated, and stuck her thumbs into the belt loops of her cut-off jeans.

'Can they do tricks, like the bottle-nose dolphins?'

'My mother's training them, and Kika,' she pointed at Kika, who was looking up with interest, 'is as clever as any bottle-nose dolphin. Most of their tricks are things that they normally do anyway, like jumping, only they learn to do them whenever the trainer gives the signal. Every time they get something right, the trainer praises them and gives them a fish. Trainers don't use the word "trick", because it makes the dolphins sound like performing pets. They say "behaviour" instead.'

Vicky's in her element, thought Daniel as he trundled a wheelbarrow full of fish along the pier. He was both envious of her self-confidence and irritated by the way she showed off. She left the group to tell him that Antonio had said they could go to the Bell Reef the next day. Daniel was already beginning to regret teaming up with her, and was uncommunicative.

Vicky found him boring and wandered back to the cabin looking for something to do. Jane looked cool, wrapped in a green cotton sarong. She was absorbed in her notes, and in no mood to be distracted.

'Why not get some homework out of the way?' she suggested.

'It's only Sunday ... oh, well, I might as

well. I need lots of space for the geometry. I'll do it on one of the restaurant tables after lunch,' said Vicky.

She liked drawing diagrams. It was neat, precise work, very satisfying. She was busy measuring angles when a big bearded man in red shorts approached her. He himself was reddish too, and his chest and legs were covered with curly ginger hair.

'Hi, I'm Ray Macdonald. Is Antonio Silva around?'

Vicky directed him to the aquarium, and he returned with Antonio a few minutes later. They sat at a table close by, drinking beer and talking. Vicky decided it must be serious business when she saw Antonio take his orange baseball cap off. Normally, it stayed glued to his head unless he went into the sea.

'I was hoping you'd be able to help. We need a base out here: somewhere we can get food and fresh water, and keep our compressor and other equipment. We'd be off in the boat most of the day, and sleep the night here now and then. You seem to have plenty of room. Of course, we'd pay for everything,' said Macdonald.

Antonio, who was normally very generous in offering hospitality, didn't seem keen. He tipped his beer glass this way and that, examining it. 'Perhaps you could explain in

41

more detail where you're planning to dive, what you're going to be doing.'

'Well, we'll start off on the Treasure Banks and move around the islands. To be honest, exactly where we dive will depend partly on what we find.' Vicky was listening to every word by this time. 'It's scientific work – we've got instruments for taking samples and checking pollution levels.' Macdonald leaned forward, elbows on the table, trying to be persuasive. 'The refinery people need to show that the new oil terminal doesn't cause any extra contamination problems, or they'll have the ecologists on the warpath.'

'They'd have me on the warpath too, if I thought the terminal was going to affect the islands. Hmmm . . . I had thought you might be after the *San José*,' said Antonio, watching for a reaction.

'For heaven's sake, where did you hear that?' The big man was disconcerted. 'Of course, the *San José* is supposed to be somewhere near the Treasure Banks, maybe that's the connection.' He paused, lit a cigarette, and scratched his hairy chest. 'I understand the Colombian navy patrols the area. Do you ever see them?'

'Occasionally,' answered Antonio, still playing with his beer glass. He was thinking that Macdonald hadn't actually denied he was interested in the *San José*; also, that if the refinery wanted to measure pollution in the islands, Vicky's father would have discussed it with him.

'I'm afraid we've hardly enough fresh water for ourselves and the restaurant,' continued Antonio. He turned aside to Vicky, who was no longer even pretending to work on her geometry, and winked at her with the eye Macdonald couldn't see. 'When did you last have a shower, Vicky?'

'A shower? Oh . . . in Cartagena.' She shook sand and salt out of her untidy hair to emphasise the point. 'And I haven't even drunk a glass of water here!'

'I can't promise that your equipment would be safe either; it'd be better if you found somwhere else.' Antonio said this in a voice that implied he wasn't going to reconsider, and put his cap on.

Macdonald grinned and shrugged. 'Okay, it's your island.'

They walked out towards the dock.

'How did you know I hadn't had a shower?' asked Vicky when Antonio reappeared, rather preoccupied. 'I only ever drink fruit juice, so it was true about the glass of water too. Why don't you want him here? Didn't you believe him?'

Antonio explained why he didn't believe Macdonald, and Vicky said, 'But if they stayed

44

on the island, you'd be able to keep track of them.'

'Look, they could be up to anything – treasure hunting, drug smuggling, stealing plants and animals from the national park ... I don't want anyone to think they've got my approval. If I find they're okay, I can always change my mind. Now, why don't you get on with your homework and let me mend the fence; those wretched turtles have been tearing it apart again.'

Daniel, who had seen Macdonald's boat leave, came in, all agog to hear what had happened, and picked up the last part of the conversation. It suddenly occurred to him that Macdonald might also be planning to explore the Bell Reef.

5 Monday morning: back to the reef

It was a perfect day for another trip to the reef. As well as masks and flippers, Vicky and Daniel collected up a shrimping net, fishing-line and hooks, a large tub, some plastic bags, a knife, plenty of bait and a pair of gloves.

'This is quite an expedition,' said Jane as she pushed them off. 'Promise me you won't let go of the boat's painter for even a moment. And if the wind gets up come back immediately.' She wondered if she was right to let them go alone, but Daniel was as comfortable on the sea as on land. It made a pleasant change to see them doing something together, instead of avoiding each other.

They had passed the last island and the boat was throwing out a strong bow-wave when a group of spotted dolphins burst out of the sea around them. Racing to keep up, the sleek grey-brown bodies criss-crossed back and forth under the hull, then porpoised alongside the boat. Daniel slowed slightly and Vicky leant out over the bow to watch the dolphins riding just ahead of the wave. They disappeared as quickly as they had come, leaving Vicky longing for more.

A few minutes later Daniel realised they must be beyond the reef. He circled and headed back, keeping further north. As before, the change in the colour of the sea showed they were in shallower water.

'We'll start near the middle of the reef. We'll have to swim into the current some of the time so we don't drift too far,' said Daniel. 'I want to see what I can catch while the tide's low. It's best to use a plastic bag full of water so the fish can't rub against the side. Will you help?'

'Sure ... but what about the noise, and that reflection, or whatever it was ... can't we check that end first?'

'It's more practical this way.' Daniel was reluctant to admit that he felt nervous about the spooky part of the reef, and preferred to get into the sea further up. He was surprised at Vicky; she had had such a fright, yet she seemed so keen to go back. 'We'll drift along anyway.'

Clutching a large clear plastic bag and some bait, Daniel swam out with the painter. As soon as he'd settled his mask he saw a small school of yellowtail snapper hovering on the top of the reef. He pointed and signalled to Vicky that she should stay on the surface; he took a deep breath and glided down towards them with as little movement as possible, holding out the bait. Although they didn't seem disturbed, the fish kept just out of reach. He tried three times before one came near: he held the bait in his left hand, and when the fish came forward to nibble he tried to jerk the plastic bag over it from behind; but the plastic was too fine, and it crumpled and stuck together, letting the fish escape.

'I'm going to put the net inside the plastic bag,' he said to Vicky. 'That should help keep the mouth of the bag open.' It was more awkward to hold in one hand, but the bag billowed out satisfactorily. The snapper had gone, and Daniel waited until he saw a pair of very pretty butterfly-fish. They were silvery-grey and yellow, with a black stripe running down over one eye and a black spot near the tail. He dived down until he was off to one side, just ahead of them, then let the bait fall. The fish swam forward, and Daniel swooped the net down. At the last moment he decided to aim for the bigger one, rather than try for the two; but to his delight he found they were both inside the bag.

Vicky helped him take the catch back on to the boat. They filled the tub with sea-water, then lowered the net and bag into it so the fish could swim out on their own, without hurting their fins or destroying the thin layer of slime which protected their bodies.

'There are some enormous lobsters hidden in crevices along the reef,' said Vicky. 'I could see their antennae waving around. Would you be able to dive deep enough to grab one?'

'I probably could, but where would we put it? It'd attack the butterfly-fish in the tub.' Daniel had assumed the lobster was meant for the aquarium collection, but Vicky was thinking of her stomach.

'It'll be all right if we throw water on it, and Mum and I can have it for supper.'

'Well . . . okay,' agreed Daniel. 'I'll put on the gloves. You keep the net ready. By the way, you haven't heard any noises have you?'

She shook her head. If anything, the water was even clearer than it had been two days ago, and the colours seemed stronger. Vicky could follow the intricate pattern of grooves covering the dome-shaped brain coral, even though she was about twenty feet above. She watched Daniel put his arm in under a ledge and draw it back quickly. He surfaced for air, shaking his wrist up and down, and showed her the place where a sea-urchin's spines had punctured the skin.

The gentle ocean swell had been carrying the boat south-east. By now they were quite near the end of the reef, and Vicky was less interested in lobsters.

'It must have been about here that we saw that gleam. Let's look along the edge. I want to go down too.'

'Well,' said Daniel responsibly, 'one of us should always be up here, just in case. We'll take turns.'

Vicky jack-knifed down towards the sharp, spiky outcrops of coral, using her arms and legs as powerfully as she could. When she was level with the top of the reef, she began to swim along, but she was already almost out of breath, and had to go back to the surface. 'It's hopeless, I can't stay under long enough. I'll have to practise,' she panted.

'You swim too hard, and use up more breath that way,' said Daniel. 'Try gliding instead – and you can nearly always manage a bit more time than you realise. Remember to pop your ears too.' It was unusual for Daniel to be teaching Vicky something and it made him feel good to have her listening so attentively. He went down neatly, coasting along the outside of the reef so he could see the sandy bottom, another thirty feet deeper.

Vicky floated, feeling the sun beating on her head and shoulders. She scanned sideways and behind her, checking for any unusual light – and for any dark shadow. Although she'd been told repeatedly that there weren't many sharks in the area, let alone bloodthirsty ones which might attack people, she always dreaded seeing a fully grown one. It made being on an ocean reef a little scary, and a little more exciting – especially afterwards. For the moment the largest fish she could see was an ugly, but not unfriendly looking, brown and white grouper.

When Daniel came up, she tried diving more smoothly, and found she had longer to look. The sunlight reached well down, but the deeper the water the more difficult it was to distinguish shades of red and orange; everything became so blue. Vicky waited until what she thought must be the last moment before turning upwards; and it was precisely then that something seemed to wink at her from the sand far below. She reached Daniel gasping: 'Did you see something? Away from the edge of the reef, on the sand?'

Daniel shook his head. 'No, but you were near that big starfish when you came up. I'll aim for that.'

He *must* solve this mystery, he thought; it was so maddening. He sucked in air and swam down the side of the reef, past the starfish, examining the bottom. It was thick with rocks and plants and shell clusters which made it more difficult to search from above. But suddenly a yellowy glow shone out from

51

the sand. A gold coin! No, this was much bigger; he was at least twenty feet from the sea-bed. A gold disk of some kind – perhaps jewellery? Wow! he thought as he shot up, he'd prayed for gold, but it still seemed incredible.

'What is it, could you see?' asked Vicky.

'I'm sure it's gold; something roundish, maybe a brooch or a pendant. I don't think I can go deep enough to get it, though. Just a minute and I'll have a try.'

'It's my turn anyway, at least I can have a look.' And Vicky put all her effort into a dive towards the bottom. She could see the disk; there seemed to be a design on it too.

'I think it's a pendant,' she puffed when she reappeared. 'But I can't see a chain or anything. Oh no!' she wailed. 'I bet it's just something dropped off a boat last week!'

After another trip down Daniel was beginning to feel chilly. He agreed it might be a pendant, and suggested the design on the outside was a cross.

'We could try fishing it up,' said Vicky, who had realised that Daniel would never reach the bottom without an air tank.

They went back to the boat to rummage through their equipment. The fishing-line was some forty feet long. Daniel wound it round his clasp knife and knotted it firmly, leaving an extra foot or so on the end; to this he attached the strongest hook. 'If I do a shallow dive, the hook should reach the sand and the weight of the knife will keep it steady,' he said. 'If there's a rough edge, or a loop for hanging the pendant, we may be able to get it. First I'll move the boat back on to the reef.' He started the engine and drove into the swell, which was building up. 'We can't stay too much longer,' Daniel was looking at his watch, which was almost as important to him as his canoe. 'I must be back for training at eleven thirty.'

The starfish hadn't moved, and was a useful landmark. Daniel unravelled the line, letting it fall to its full length, and held it above the gold disk. They could just see it from the surface, now that they knew where to look. Daniel swam down a little way, allowing the hook to scrape the sand. But it was very difficult to control the line: the knife swung around in the current, the hook wasn't heavy enough, and returning to the surface for air made the operation very inefficient.

'Why don't I come down and take the line when you need to breathe,' said Vicky. 'Then it'll be nearer the right place, and there'll be more chance of hooking the disk. ... Or, I know, we can tie the line on to the end of the painter and dangle it from up here!'

Daniel thought about the painter and pointed out that the swell was so strong it would be even worse fishing from the surface. 'You swim down and take over when I signal. But don't drop my knife whatever you do.'

This system was a bit better, and they managed to shift the disk, which lay between two rocks. Daniel went down deep once again, and reported that he thought he could see a small hole in the disk, as well as something else sticking out beside it.

Although they were both exhausted, it seemed worth trying again. At the next changeover, when Vicky took the line from Daniel, she felt the hook tugging – it was caught under the disk. Suddenly, the same ear-splitting clanging as before rang across the reef; once again, Vicky felt jarred, as though by a terrific shock. She was dazed and scared, and it took a second to realise she was no longer holding on to the line. Dismayed, she swam up to Daniel. For once, she was wordless.

'I heard the noise; you dropped the line.' Daniel sounded cross.

'I'm awfully sorry. But wasn't that clang something! I can hardly hear now. What can it be?'

'It didn't sound so loud to me. I'm going to see if the line is within reach, or if it went down to the bottom. Then we must go.'

Feeling very trembly, Vicky put her snorkel back in her mouth and ducked to watch. He

54

just couldn't have heard what she had. The sky was clouding over, and without sunlight the reef seemed ghostly. The knife was down by the disk, but Daniel would never find the line. Wait a minute, there it was, further along; no, that wasn't a fishing-line, it was a thick rope snaking out from a pile of coral off the main reef. Vicky was puzzling this out when another clang struck through the water. It didn't sound anything like as loud or as frightening from the surface; but Daniel must have felt the full effect, because she had never seen him zoom up so fast.

'Come on back to the boat,' he called.

Relieved that she'd remembered to hang on to the painter through all the drama, Vicky swam round to the stern and got aboard.

'I understand what you meant now. It's just tremendous when you're down there. I'm sorry I was annoyed about the knife,' said Daniel. He looked shivery, and his dark skin had gone muddy-grey.

'What about that rope?' asked Vicky.

'I don't know. It's all a bit of a muddle. I saw the rope and I looked up thinking it was the painter, but of course the painter's yellow. Anyway, I looked down, and the rope went to a mound covered with coral.' Vicky nodded. 'Then that terrifying noise began, and I could only think about getting away.' Daniel hesitated. 'You know, I'm almost sure the mound rocked a tiny bit.'

They spent a few minutes recovering, and discussing the noise, the rope, the mound and the gold disk, until Daniel said, 'Look, we have to race back. We can talk later.' And the boat roared away from the reef, slopping water out of the tub and leaving the precious butterfly-fish practically stranded.

6 Monday afternoon: the headless man

Jane was still at her notes. She hoped to publish an article on the training of the Sotalia dolphins: very few had ever been kept in captivity and taught to perform in shows.

'You're not your usual cheerful self this afternoon. Did you enjoy the trip? Were the ghosts out haunting?' Jane flapped her arms and said, 'Oooh-oooh' into the mirror that hung on the wall in front of her desk.

'Don't be silly, Mum.' Vicky had been wondering whether to tell her everything, but Jane's playfulness put her off. She didn't want to be teased about the reef. She helped herself to melon juice from the kitchen and took a coke out to Daniel; he was on the end of the pier, gazing at the dolphins without noticing them.

They went over all the details they could think of: the fish didn't seem to be affected by the noise – the reef was extraordinarily rich in marine life, perhaps because the local fishermen didn't like going there, said Daniel. The gold – was it the same bright light they'd glimpsed on the first trip? It glinted, but not as strongly as they'd remembered. Was it a disk or pendant, old or new? Gold was about the only thing that wasn't corroded by the sea, however long it stayed underwater, volunteered Vicky (she'd learned that from a magazine). And if there was more gold alongside the disk, did it mean there was a whole treasure trove? As for the rope, had it been there all along and only floated up when a current shifted it? So far, they'd come up with a lot of questions and very few answers.

Nobody had ever mentioned a shipwreck on that reef, Daniel said. In fact people didn't even want to talk about the Bell Reef. Maybe the ship's bell had been ringing when it sank. Did Vicky believe in ghosts? he asked, afraid she might laugh at him.

'I suppose I do in a way. But I don't believe they could actually do anything, like ring a bell. If there's a bell there, it could start jangling whenever the sea moves it.' Her matter-of-fact mind chose the obvious explanation, though she thought a ghost would have been more fun. 'Do you really think it's a shipwreck?'

'Yes, I do. Somehow the bell makes it even more likely; my grandfather used to tell me so many stories about haunted wrecks. He says people who go after treasure have bad luck because gold carries evil in it. Gold used to be mined by black slaves and mountain Indians; who knows, maybe even some of my ancestors. The Spaniards didn't care about the people they found living here, and they melted down the beautiful gold ornaments and jewellery they'd made.' Daniel shifted back to the original question. 'Anyway, imagine all the people who must have drowned in ships around these islands – of course there would be ghosts.'

Vicky was astounded. It was the first time she'd heard an islander say anything like this. They were sometimes quiet, and sometimes very lively; she found them pleasant to chat with, but had never imagined they might have ideas about anything except fishing. Islanders weren't educated and didn't travel far, in contrast with her schoolfriends, who disappeared to Miami and Europe for the holidays.

'If I knew how to use scuba gear, it'd be easy to get down to the bottom. I suppose we'll have to tell a diver the whole story,' said Daniel glumly.

'They have divers at the oil terminal,' suggested Vicky.

'Yes, but one of them's Ray Macdonald. Antonio doesn't trust him. Anyone like that would just take what he found for himself.'

Frustrated by their helplessness, they sat and

watched Kika scratching her back against the sandy bottom.

There must be some way of finding out about the reef without actually diving there, mused Vicky. Her friend was always talking about researching things; her father was a historian . . .

'Hey, that's it, there *is* something I can try! My friend's father works in that library in the main square in Cartagena. He studies all the old documents, and writes about the Spanish empire – at least, I think that's right. I can ask him if there's any record of a shipwreck on the Bell Reef.' Vicky was delighted with her idea, and found Daniel's half-hearted response most annoying.

'I've got to write a story on pirates and Cartagena for my history class. I can say I need to go to the library to look things up . . . I'll go and ask Mum right now.'

Jane was suspicious about Vicky's sudden enthusiasm for history: she'd always said she thought writing was a bore, and numbers were much easier. 'What's all this about pirates? Well, it'll keep you out of my hair, anyway. You can go in the restaurant boat – I think Tuesday's the day they go in to Cartagena to stock up. Actually, you can collect a couple of things from the flat for me, and call Dad and see if you can persuade him to come out this weekend.'

Antonio confirmed the boat would be going. 'I'll ask Pedro to walk as far as the library with you ... no ... ' He wouldn't listen to Vicky's protest. 'It's better that way, I'll feel happier; I want him to take a letter to the naval base too, to warn them to check out Ray Macdonald. And if you talk to your father, ask him about the pollution story. I have a feeling it'll be news to him.'

All in all the trip would be rather useful, Vicky told Daniel. She was also hoping to buy him a new knife, provided she could winkle some money out of her parents.

'I'll ask my grandfather whether he knows anything about the reef,' said Daniel as he set off homewards. It sounded a bit feeble compared with Vicky's ambitious plans, but he had more faith in the old man's memories than Cartagena's libraries.

It was a glorious evening, and Jane and Vicky joined Antonio on his terrace to admire the sunset. His wife was in the capital, where their daughter went to college, and he didn't see her very often. He was fanatical about the aquarium and couldn't bear to give it up for city life.

Before touching the horizon, the sun disappeared behind the pier in a fiery-red haze, and feathery wisps of cloud high in the sky turned deep pink. The dolphins surfaced close to the terrace, their explosive puffs of breath breaking the stillness.

Vicky described the group of wild spotted dolphins that had joined the boat on the way to the reef.

Antonio was interested. 'I've been thinking of putting another dolphin or two in the pen. What do you think, Jane?'

'The more I train dolphins, the more I worry about keeping them in aquariums. Of course, it's not so bad here, with the sea just the other side of the fence, and the pen full of rocks and sand and small fish.'

'How about training them for a while, then opening up the fence so they could get out if they wanted?' asked Vicky.

'It might work,' said Jane thoughtfully, running her fingers through her hair. 'People aren't usually prepared to try that kind of experiment – they put a lot of money into training dolphins. Anyway, an animal that's been fed in a pool for years would have to be re-taught how to survive in the ocean. But as I said it's different here: they're close to where they were caught, and we haven't even started doing shows yet.'

'Speaking of shows, will there be any problem when you leave and Daniel and I take over the training?'

'Oh no, don't worry,' said Jane. 'Kika will perform for you as she does for me, as long

62

as you follow roughly the same rules and signs. You can try it tomorrow and see.'

'What's for supper?' Vicky wanted to know. 'We nearly got a lobster – there are some huge ones on that reef. I bet it's fish.'

They left Antonio in his house, and the smell of grilling chicken reached them long before they got to the restaurant. The cook was dozing behind the serving hatch, and some of the staff were eating in the kitchen. Vicky attacked her plateful of chicken and chips with gusto.

Half a mile away, on the other island, Daniel was settling down to some fish soup left over from lunch.

'You seem worried: nothing's happened over at the aquarium, has it?' asked his mother. The family had begun to rely on Daniel's earnings, and she didn't like the thought of him losing his job. She couldn't see any point in keeping a whole lot of fish and animals trapped in pens, but if people paid to look at them, that was a good enough reason for her.

'No, no . . . everything's fine.'

'I heard you'd taken the foreign girl out in the boat,' she said chattily. Daniel never told her much, and his mother welcomed the slightest variation in routine; she spent most of her days alone with the kids and their grandfather.

'So? I caught two fine butterfly-fish for the aquarium, and Antonio was happy. She wasn't much help though.' Daniel had forgotten how fast gossip spread in the islands. He knew he wasn't being quite fair on Vicky, but his mother always exaggerated everything. She'd want to invite Jane and Vicky over to their shack next, he thought, looking critically round at the rough plank walls and his sisters playing on the floor with the naked baby.

Daniel's grandfather was napping outside in a rocking chair which looked even older than he was. In fact, nobody had any idea how old he really was, because he had no birth certificate and he always referred to 'the winter when not a drop of water fell' or 'the year I caught a two hundred-pound green turtle' if he was asked when something had happened. He'd been very ill a few years ago, and could no longer manage a canoe. Daniel squatted beside him, wondering if the enormous halo round the moon meant it would rain.

'What is it then?' His grandfather shifted, coughed, and opened his eyes.

'Do you know a place called the Bell Reef, out in the ocean, the other side of the government island?' asked Daniel.

'Did I ever tell you the story of the headless man when you were little? No?'

Daniel settled more comfortably, realising his grandfather was going to answer in his own way.

'In the old days, when the English pirate Francis Drake captured Cartagena, he wanted a big ransom. The people collected up a lot of treasure from their secret hoards – of course they hid a lot too – and Drake sailed away with it, no doubt very pleased with himself. One of his boats needed repairs below the water-line so they landed on a sandy beach. Drake decided to bury part of his treasure behind the beach, and six sailors hauled the chest full of gold and silver and precious stones up the hill. It must have been very heavy.

'They dug a deep pit and hid the chest. Then Drake asked who would stay behind and look after it. One of the sailors was stupid enough to fall into the trap, and offered his services. Drake accused him: "So you wanted to rob me, did you?" And with his sword he cut the sailor's head off.' The old man paused for so long that Daniel looked to see whether he'd fallen asleep.

'I don't think it'll rain tomorrow,' he said, and continued. 'They sailed away, and Drake poisoned the sailors who had helped bury the treasure, one by one, until only one of them was still alive. When he was near that part of the coast again Drake decided he would pick up the treasure. But the sailor who had survived was determined to avenge his friends, and he put poison in Drake's food. The pirate was soon in agony, and very sick. Just before dying Drake saw a headless man, dripping blood, in his ship's cabin.

'The people who live near that beach often see the headless man. He waves his arms around, as though he's trying to tell them something. Then he vanishes. Those who search for the treasure are always scared off by the headless man.'

'Nobody's ever found it, then?' asked Daniel.

'Nobody's found it. And it was greed for gold that caused those deaths, and many, many others too. There are lessons to be learned from these old tales ... So don't you go disturbing the dead by poking around on the Bell Reef.'

'But, Grandfather, I don't understand. Do you mean there really is a ship with treasure wrecked there?'

'It's not just a shipwreck. Keep away.' And Daniel's grandfather wouldn't tell him any more.

7   Tuesday: the library

The restaurant boat – a long sturdy motor canoe – left early; by eight thirty they were already passing Cartagena's beach-front skyscrapers and the naval base. Vicky put on pink cotton trousers and floppy pink tee-shirt over her bathing suit. She didn't think the library would be open until at least nine o'clock, so she went with Pedro to deliver Antonio's letter to Captain Mendoza. Pedro was explaining their errand to navy guards at the barrier when a jeep drew up, hooting impatiently. 'That's the Captain,' said someone, and they hurried over.

Brisk and neat in a crisp white uniform, he took the letter. 'Tell Don Antonio that I expect to be out in the islands tomorrow or the next day. Good-day to you both.' He nodded at them and the jeep roared into the base.

The huge iron-studded library doors creaked open, and Vicky found she was the first visitor of the day. Her friend's father, Mr Torres, hadn't arrived so she sat down on a massive iron cannon mounted in the courtyard. Perhaps they'd find one of these at the bottom of the reef, she thought.

Mr Torres came bustling into the yard, and looked short-sightedly at her. Pulling at his untidy black moustache, he said: 'It's Vicky, isn't it? How well you look! You're taller every time I see you. What a surprise. Are you looking for me? Come along into my office.'

He had a large, dark room lined with shelves of books and bundles of papers tied up with red ribbons. Two old maps hung on the wall behind his desk. One showed Cartagena Bay and its defences, the other traced the route taken by the treasure fleets. The only modern thing in the room was a photocopying machine.

'I'm just getting the historical society's journal ready for publication. These manuscripts have to be at the printer's this afternoon, so I'm rather busy. What can I do for you?'

'Well . . . ' Vicky gulped. 'How do I get information on old wrecks in the islands? Are there any maps or records or anything like that?'

'Goodness me, you haven't taken up treasure hunting, have you? The strangest people come in here and ask these questions. It's not easy, you know, there are no lists or anything. You have to read the old documents carefully, and piece together clues about battles, storms, the galleon fleets and so on. Most of the details are hidden away in lengthy official reports or letters written by governors, admirals and bureaucrats. Do you know what dates you're after? The papers are usually filed by the year.'

Vicky didn't know what to reply. She had no idea of the date. So she came up with the one wreck everyone had heard of: 'About the time of the *San José*.'

'1708? Luckily that period has been quite well researched; of course you won't find so much detail in modern histories but at least you'll be able to read them. The original documents are written in an old script – even experts like myself have difficulty understanding it.'

He rummaged around on his desk and unearthed one of the historical society's journals. 'We published a long article on the eighteenth-century treasure fleets – there weren't many by that time – and there's quite a bit about the *San José* too. You can learn a lot from this. But, Vicky,' he looked at her closely, wondering what island fantasies she'd created, 'it's no good thinking you'll be able to pinpoint wrecks.'

'Supposing I already knew *where* it was and wanted to find out *what* it was?' Her library search no longer seemed such a brilliant idea to Vicky.

'Ah, that's different.' Mr Torres tugged at both ends of his moustache, until he realised that Vicky was watching, fascinated. 'In that case the first thing to do is study the wreck itself and the objects on the sea-bed around it – anchors, cannon, weapons, coins; any of those things would be a good guide to the date and origin of the ship. From then on it's much easier. Mind you, you need a permit for that sort of work.' Someone carrying a pile of papers pushed the door open. 'Look, I must get down to this. Take the journal into the library to read and ask the librarian to show you the books covering the colonial period in Cartagena. I'll see you later.'

Vicky wasn't over-eager to read the article, but she thought she'd better not disappoint him, and sat down at a table in the library. She learned that the *San José* had been sunk by the English navy and that it was one of the richest prizes in the world. It was discouraging reading because the language was difficult, and for all she knew their wreck could be fifty or 450 years old. She glanced at the library section on colonial history, thoroughly disheartened. Most of the books had the dullest titles, like *Cartagena, a history from the foundation to 1800*. She picked out the two which looked most interesting: one on tales and traditions of Cartagena, the other on pirates of the Spanish Main.

She made a few notes on pirates for her essay

and began to leaf through the book on tales and traditions. This was much more fun – there were lots of ghost stories. The introduction said the author had gathered all the material by talking to people in and around Cartagena. One story was about a woman in white who tricked children into jumping down a well to keep her drowned daughter company; another described a large brightly lit steamer which rammed fishing boats at night.

Then she saw something which made her wriggle with excitement – a story called 'The Bell Reef'. It began: 'An island fisherman once told this author a tale fit to chill the blood of any man. The fisherman was old, weak and near to dying. He needed much persuasion to speak and only did so because, he said, it was not right for such a warning as that contained in the tale to die with him.'

Vicky found she'd been holding her breath. She looked up and saw the library was now full of people reading newspapers and studying. Some of them looked half-asleep, as if they'd come in for a nap. It was unpleasantly hot with no air-conditioning; the librarian had the only fan on his own desk. She would have liked a drink but she couldn't bear to leave the story.

'In the days when Cartagena was a rich city, and the Spanish fleets anchored in the bay before proceeding to Portobelo for their treasure cargoes, many slaves were imported from Africa. They were crammed into the holds of Dutch, Spanish, English, French and Portuguese ships, and thousands died on the two-month journey. Some ships had official licences for this terrible traffic, but the slave business was too profitable for the smugglers to ignore.

'One of these smugglers was a Frenchman. He began to trade slaves early in the eighteenth century at a time when Cartagena was ruled by a stern man; the governor was determined to stop contraband, and even went so far as to throw a slave trafficker into prison and confiscate his goods. Few African slaves reached Cartagena during this period, so they fetched excellent prices for the smugglers willing to risk the trip.'

'I see you're hard at work.' The voice made Vicky jump. She turned round and recognised Ray Macdonald peering over her shoulder. 'What's got you so fascinated?' He made it sound like an accusation.

As casually as possible, she said, 'Oh, just some ghost stories.'

Macdonald grinned – a really cheesy grin, thought Vicky. 'The professor in there told me you had the journal with the piece on the *San José*. I didn't think that could be quite so gripping. D'you mind if I take it?'

Vicky was relieved he didn't show any interest in the ghost stories. But it was bad enough that he'd come to the library. If he nosed around the shelves he'd probably find the book on tales and tradition . . . he might even look through it. She went on reading.

'The Frenchman arrived near Cartagena in a ship packed with four hundred African slaves – some say more and some say less. In a deserted bay he handed over 150 slaves to a dealer, and was paid in gold and silver. Then he set sail for Portobelo with the rest. The weather soon turned foul, with howling winds ripping through the rigging and mountainous waves tossing the ship hither and thither over the Treasure Banks.'

People around Vicky were getting up and putting things away; she was horrified to see it was already midday. The library was closing for lunch, and she was supposed to be back on the dock at three. How was she to finish the story? It was a reference library, not a lending one. If only she'd thought of photocopying the pages a bit earlier! But perhaps there would just be time in the afternoon. A notice on the librarian's desk gave the afternoon opening hours: 2.30 p.m. to 6.00 p.m. Thank goodness, thought Vicky, I'll be here at 2.30 on the dot, photocopy the story, and dash to the boat.

She pushed her way through the lunch-time

crowds on the shady side of the street. Balconies laden with lush plants overhung the pavement, and flowering trees grew in some of the courtyards. Most of the old buildings had been altered to make shops, offices and snack-bars. But now and then Vicky glimpsed a family sitting down to lunch at a lace-covered table, or a humped figure swinging in a hammock. She reached the flat in a few minutes. Rosa, delighted, threw her arms round Vicky and invited her to lunch.

'I must call Dad first.' She rang the refinery, but her father was out at the terminal for the day, said a secretary. Vicky was disappointed. She knew he wouldn't like it if she asked someone else about Ray Macdonald or the pollution study.

They went downstairs, and Rosa gave her a plate loaded with coconut rice, fried bananas and a large piece of fish smothered in tomatoes and peppers. She sat down to keep Vicky company, saying she would eat later. It was always restful being with Rosa; she never fussed about unimportant things, like tidying Vicky's hair.

'Your father has been working very hard, I think. But he told me he'd be going out to the island for the weekend. Are you having fun with the dolphins?' Normally Vicky talked about nothing else after being on the island. Jane had once asked Rosa if she'd like to take the day trip out, but Rosa had been embarrassed and said she was scared stiff of the sea. Vicky asked where her children were – both were younger than Vicky, but she was fond of them and helped them with their sums. An aunt had taken them to the beach. 'They'll be sizzling on the sand,' laughed Rosa.

Vicky went up to collect the things that Jane wanted from the flat. She also took her own Swiss army knife – it wasn't anything like as strong as Daniel's knife but it was the best she could do until she had enough money to buy him another. A package on the kitchen table caught her eye. She peeked in one end and saw a large black and red torch; certain it was the one Daniel had asked for, she took that too. She promised Rosa that she wouldn't talk to any strangers and set off for the library.

Along the way she bought some shampoo for Jane, and by 2.20 she was sitting at the foot of a statue in the main square, waiting for the library doors to open. Two businessmen on the bench opposite were having their shoes cleaned. A boy with an ice-cream cart tried to sell her a strawberry-flavoured cone, which she resisted, because she didn't want sticky fingers. It was the hottest part of the day and nobody was moving unnecessarily. At 2.40 the heavy doors were still shut. At 2.50 Vicky was banging on them as hard as she could, and people in the square were watching with amusement. Infuriated, she asked a bank guard nearby what time the library would open.

'Who knows,' he said. 'Maybe any minute, maybe in an hour, maybe tomorrow.'

She stomped impatiently up and down, getting hotter and stickier every minute. A uniformed doorman lounging outside the hotel the other side of the square beckoned her. 'They may have gone to the funeral – the director's sister-in-law died,' he said. 'Come back another day.'

'But it's *got* to be today,' wailed Vicky, almost in tears. The doorman shrugged. When a church clock struck 3.15 Vicky reluctantly decided to go and meet Pedro; it wasn't likely he'd leave without her, but Antonio had given him strict instructions not to dawdle. Of all the things to happen . . . I bet that rotten librarian is having his afternoon nap; he couldn't possibly care about the director's sister-in-law, she thought as she ran to the waterfront.

'Come on, come on,' called Pedro. 'I have to pick up the mail at the marina on the way out. Let's get going.'

Vicky was furious with the world and disgusted with herself. She'd found the vital clue, and lost it, and she had nothing that would impress Daniel.

8 Wednesday: Kika performs

'Can I give Daniel the torch now, or should I wait until Dad comes?' Vicky and Jane were eating paw-paw after the early morning training session.

'I don't think Dad would mind – as long as you're sure it's meant for Daniel. But let him get the fish done first.' Jane stretched her arms above her head. 'I'll be glad when all this writing's over. I wonder whether Antonio has a typewriter here . . . why, you thieving bird!' This was aimed at one of the parrots, which had sneaked a piece of paw-paw off her plate.

Vicky sat on the cooler, her long legs dangling over the sea, waiting for Daniel to finish his chores. Whenever she shifted position, the hot plastic burned the backs of her thighs. Two small canoes were out over the reef that circled the bay. Half closing her eyes against the glare, she could see two snorkels moving along the ruffled surface like periscopes, disappearing now and then. The island fishermen often worked this way: one would stay in the canoe while the other swam

78

up and down the reef with a spear or a net. She heard someone laughing as one of the snorkellers tossed a lobster into a canoe. He would sell it to the restaurant later.

There was one disadvantage to having private conversations in such a public place, thought Daniel when he saw the fishermen. Luis, Pedro and the other islanders were already making sly remarks about the amount of time he and Vicky spent talking together.

Vicky jumped off the cooler so he could heave the fish in. She handed him a package: 'Open it. It's from Dad really.'

Exactly what he'd wanted: red and black, completely waterproof, a strong beam and a handle on top – it even had batteries in it. 'Fantastic!' said Daniel. 'Did you see your father?'

'No.' Vicky wrinkled her nose and made a face. 'I didn't even talk to him. And you can't imagine what happened at the library.' She described her frustrations. 'Of course, I can go and read the story after half-term but that may be too late . . . '

'It was about slaves?' mused Daniel. Then he told her what his grandfather had said. Vicky tried to remember the dates she'd seen.

'The Bell Reef story said something about the eighteenth century – and I know Francis Drake sacked Cartagena in 1586, because I noted it for my essay. So what's Francis Drake got to do with all this?'

'No, you missed the point,' said Daniel. 'Grandfather didn't mean Drake was there or anything like that – it was just an example to tell me something. The problem is, I'm still not sure what he was getting at.'

'Well . . . ' Vicky thought for a moment. 'There's got to be a wreck there, and it could be something to do with a slave ship. We still don't know if there's a real bell, though, or why everyone's so scared of the reef, apart from the noise.'

'Or if there's lots of gold there,' added Daniel. 'We'll have to go back and try to fish something up.'

'It's easy enough to say that – how?' Vicky bent over the edge of the pier to see what Kika had got hold of: 'It's okay, it's only a stick.'

'Vicky.' She turned sharply – it was the first time Daniel had ever used her name. He was staring at Kika. 'I know the way. Kika can do it.'

'What?' she exclaimed, then laughed. 'Sure, dolphins can pick things up, but they have to be trained to do it.'

'No, no, she already knows how. She seemed to cotton on right away.' Daniel explained how he'd dropped the whistle and Kika had retrieved it. 'Look, I'll show you.' He fetched the whistle, suddenly feeling nervous about the test. If Kika didn't respond he'd look awfully stupid. He waited until Kika next came up, one eye on them, and threw the whistle close to her. She twirled round, diving down after it, and came straight back holding it in her mouth. The only problem was, she refused to give it up, and swam off round the pen. Much to their relief, she dropped it on to the training platform.

'She's really smart, isn't she?' said Vicky. 'If we had a fish for her she'd probably give us the whistle. Let's try.'

It worked perfectly. Kika was used to the reward system. She rolled sideways and started waving a flipper at them, in the hope of another fish.

'Wait a minute . . . how would she know *what* to pick up if we didn't throw it in?' Vicky's question stumped them both.

'What do they do in shows? Does the trainer always throw something?' Daniel had never seen a dolphin show.

'Yes . . . I think so. But I think there could be another way too. Mum has lots of books and papers on dolphin behaviour, I'll have a look.'

Kika was still floating at the surface, waiting for more entertainment.

'It's a crazy idea anyway; we'd have to get her out of the pen and persuade her to follow

the boat all that way. Jane would never let us
. . . ' Daniel's voice dropped as Jane came out
along the pier.

'Don't you realise it's nearly eleven thirty,
you chatterboxes? Where's the fish then?'

They leaped up guiltily and started filling
the buckets. As soon as training began, Vicky
rushed off to the cabin to see if she could
find any useful hints in her mother's dolphin
literature.

Kika sailed through the hoop, earning her last
fish; Jane knelt down beside Daniel to help feed
Pacho and Molly. Daniel took the opportunity
to bring up some of the questions which were
bothering him; he had to keep his Spanish as
simple as possible for Jane.

'Why doesn't Kika jump over the fence
to the sea? She could, couldn't she?'

Jane nodded. 'Yes she could – but she's
probably too frightened to risk it. If I told
her to, she would. But . . . ' she fumbled for
words in Spanish ' . . . it would be dangerous
for her. Later she might try it on her own . . .
the sea goes up and down' (she meant the tide)
'and she wouldn't know how high the fence
was.'

Daniel reflected how seriously Jane treated
any query about the dolphins, and how easy-
going she was at other times. It seemed a
terrible betrayal even to consider taking Kika

to the reef. 'If she went out to sea, would she come back?' he asked.

'I'm sure she would,' said Jane. 'This is her place now, she has food here, she feels safe, and she has companions – dolphins and humans.'

It would be too obvious if he led on to something else: for example, whether Kika would stay with a boat in the open sea. Perhaps he could introduce that later, thought Daniel.

When Jane had gone, he swam along the fence examining the wire mesh to see how it was fastened to the metal uprights. It appeared to be all one piece up to the last pole before the pier. Here there was a break; someone had probably miscalculated the length of the fence and they'd had to add on one more section. The two sets of mesh were laced to each other, and to the pole, with short bits of wire.

It wouldn't be too difficult to free one side for, say, the last five feet down to the bottom. Unless somebody swam down especially to inspect the fence, it wouldn't be noticed. Daniel would leave a bit of wire holding the mesh to the pole right at the bottom; when that was freed, he'd be able to lift the mesh, making a hole big enough for Kika to swim through.

Visitors were trickling into the aquarium, signalling the arrival of the big tourist boat.

Daniel went to find his father, who usually stayed on board to look after the boat. His mother had sent a shopping list of things she wanted brought out from Cartagena, and Daniel himself needed some shorts – he hardly ever wore any other clothes.

'Everyone at home all right?' asked his father, short-tempered as always. 'How does she think I'm going to get all this on my wages? Well . . . I'll see.'

Daniel looked at the way his father's belly hung over his khaki trousers, and decided most of his wages were probably spent on beer. Life was a lot quieter at home without him; his mother might be lonely, but Daniel thought she seemed a lot happier.

Vicky and Daniel met for another conference before lunch, each reporting progress. They tried in vain to think of some other way of reaching the objects on the sea-bed. There was no alternative: Kika had to join the team. It was terribly risky, but as they worked out the details, the advantages of including Kika seemed greater and greater. Not only could she dive deep, but her radar-like echo-location system was perfect for poor light or murky water.

Vicky thought she could teach Kika to find an object similar to one she was shown: for example, if they showed her a coin and gave her a signal – gesturing downwards would be the easiest – she would look for a coin. They might have to try several times, but it shouldn't be too difficult. After all, dolphins used clicking sounds to hunt fish all the time. The echoes from the clicks told them exactly what was in the water around them.

Daniel resented the way Vicky took over the whole project when it was he who had discovered Kika's skill. On the other hand, he recognised that there was a special under-standing between Vicky and Kika, which would speed everything up. He said the fence presented no problem – except for persuading Kika to swim through, and then go with them to the reef. They agreed Vicky should coax her – probably with fish. In fact, it would be best if she had very little food on the day so she'd be hungry. That led them to another question: when should it be?

Kika couldn't leave the pen during the day without Jane knowing. They'd have to go after dark. Once or twice Jane and Vicky had been on night fishing trips with Antonio; there didn't seem any reason why she and Daniel shouldn't arrange one.

They chose the following night – Thursday; if something went wrong, they could always put it off until Friday. Meanwhile, they must get organised and work with Kika. Vicky thought a moonlight swim with the dolphins would be a good excuse for testing her on pick-ups in the dark.

During the afternoon, Daniel had several panic-stricken moments. He would stop what he was doing, and think of all the ghastly things that could go wrong. The worst would be if they lost Kika. Well, if she went off, it would show she wasn't content in the aquarium, and shouldn't be kept there. But he didn't think Antonio would accept that point of view, and of course he'd lose his job. For Vicky it was all a lark – she had such faith in her own luck. It was true that if they got just that one gold disk, it would all be worthwhile.

Late in the day the wind blew up, and under cover of the waves Daniel rewired part of the fence. Once in a while he swam round the pen playing with the dolphins, in case anyone noticed him diving down again and again in the same spot. Kika was extremely curious – he could imagine her asking what he was up to. But most of the islanders were helping Antonio build a new bar near the dock, and it wasn't fishing weather. Daniel tried to think of things he might need from home, and reminded himself to warn his mother he would be out the following night.

Vicky was roaming restlessly round the cabin looking for objects which might be lying at the bottom of the reef. Obviously, she wouldn't be able to show Kika a large gold disk. What was the nearest in size and shape?

'You're driving me bananas – what do you want?' asked Jane, unable to concentrate on her writing.

'Okay, okay, I'm going,' said Vicky. She chose the largest coins she could find – ten pesos, about an inch across – and went out to the dolphins.

It was a grey, blustery evening, certainly not a night for a moonlit dip. Daniel had left plenty of fish in the cooler. She rode the float across to the platform, dropping one coin in on the way, and slapped the water to get Kika's attention. Holding the second coin in front of Kika's snout, she pointed to the sea-floor, then hid the coin. Kika swam round in a circle, showing no sign of diving. At least she looked interested.

Vicky decided to go back to the beginning. She showed Kika the coin again, only this time she threw it into the water when she signalled downwards. Kika flipped over and went down with a lot of squeaking and clicking. She brought Vicky the coin, and received a fish. They repeated it once more that way, and the next time Vicky hid the coin behind her back. Kika disappeared. Vicky bit her lip in anticipation – she was staying under longer

87

than usual. Sure enough, Kika came up with the other coin. Vicky gave her two fish and did a triumphant dance on the rocking platform.

'Kika, good girl! You're wonderful! Oh, how wonderful you are!' she sang. Kika seemed to like being praised; while she did a couple of frisky jumps to show off, Vicky threw one of the coins in on the other side of the platform. She slapped the water again, showing Kika the second coin and hiding it when she gave her signal.

Bursts of clicking noises told Vicky that Kika was scanning the bottom, sending out clicks and listening for the echo. She came up empty-mouthed, but dived straight down without trying to claim a reward. After another minute or so she was back with the coin, demanding fish. Vicky could hardly believe it had been so easy. But things would be different in the open sea at night, she thought, shivering suddenly.

9 Thursday: setting off

The sea was still choppy on Thursday morning, but Daniel's grandfather said the wind would die down by lunch-time. The weather forecast he gave the family each morning was nearly always right. Daniel was already on the pier cutting up fish when Vicky appeared in a yellow knee-length tee-shirt. She reminded him not to fill Kika's bucket too full.

'Stop ordering me around. I have a mind too, you know,' said Daniel in exasperation. There was a tense moment – he wouldn't have dreamt of saying anything like that a week ago. Then they grinned at each other and Vicky apologised.

By the time Jane had finished training, the sun was out and the waves beyond the reef had calmed to shimmering ripples. Vicky asked about the evening fishing trip over breakfast; Jane gave her a wicked smirk, and said she wouldn't mind joining them. She burst out laughing at Vicky's obvious dismay. 'Don't worry, I won't spoil your fun. But I hope you're not going too far.'

'Oh no, just the other side of the government

island,' said Vicky semi-truthfully. They were about to leave when Antonio brought three people into the restaurant for coffee; Vicky thought one of them looked familiar, and he came over to wish them good morning.

'Captain Mendoza, at your service.' He bowed over Jane's hand. 'I met your daughter the other day.' Even in shorts and bare feet he looked purposeful.

'The Captain's the best diver in Colombia,' said Antonio. 'And he's an old friend too. He makes sure treasure hunters don't strip the wrecks round here, don't you?'

Vicky stared at him, brown eyes popping. The Captain was introducing his companions, an archaeologist and another navy diver.

'We're out here to have a look at a wreck, as a matter of fact. Some company claims to have found the *San José*; no, I can't tell you exactly where, but it's very deep – nearly a thousand feet down.' He turned to Antonio. 'I got your note – delivered by this young lady – and I wondered whether you'd seen anything more of this Ray Macdonald? We've been hearing quite a bit about him, one way and another.'

'I saw him in the library in Cartagena,' said Vicky. 'He was looking for an article about the *San José*.'

'Hmmm, we can't make out what he's up

to; if the *San José*'s where we think it is, he'd need some pretty sophisticated equipment to get near it. Antonio, I'd like to take a walk round the aquarium, if you don't mind.' It was clear he wanted to talk in private.

'What will happen if it really is the *San José*? Do you just bring up the treasure?' Vicky asked the archaeologist. He was athletic and sunburnt, and looked as though he spent all his time outdoors.

He laughed. 'No, my job is to stop them doing it like that, and to make sure we learn all we can from the ship. After all, it's a historic monument for Colombia. It'll be very slow work at this depth, maybe years. The government will probably call in a specialised salvage company, and we'll keep tabs on them.'

'And the people who found the *San José*? Don't they get some of the treasure?' said Vicky anxiously.

'They receive a small share of everything that's recovered; in the case of the *San José*, the share could run into millions. But Colombia should keep objects of historical value, like old navigating instruments or rare jewellery. Have you ever noticed that there's practically nothing in Cartagena's museums?'

Vicky hadn't thought about it. But she was relieved to hear that the finders got something

– it made the Bell Reef search all the more enticing.

The Captain returned and bowed once again to Jane. 'I've just asked Antonio to a small get-together on our patrol ship this evening. Perhaps you would like to come too?'

Jane said she would be delighted, and Vicky growled to herself in annoyance – it meant Antonio would be needing his launch. Daniel's canoe was hardly fit for an ocean venture: he had made a sail out of old sacks, cut up and patched together. Vicky knew her mother would never let her go out sailing at night, and she didn't fancy paddling all the way to the reef.

But Jane had realised they would need an outboard for the fishing trip, and was arranging for Daniel to borrow the restaurant boat.

Vicky was still stuck on the gold disk problem. She had a light gold chain, and Jane wore a gold wedding ring. Neither was remotely like the big disk, and Vicky didn't think they would help Kika understand what to look for. She rambled round the storeroom and kitchen, hoping for inspiration. The lid off a biscuit tin was about the right size – but the ants would get in and eat the biscuits. That was easily solved: she took them as well as the lid.

Delving into a pile of old engine parts and

other junk behind the storeroom, Vicky found two flat iron rings like giant washers. They would be good for practising, she thought, and went out to make sure that Kika remembered the pick-up signal.

Not wanting to give Kika any more food than necessary, Vicky took half a fish for the reward. Kika had no trouble finding the washer Vicky dropped in, even though it was quite a bit smaller than the one shown her.

The conspirators had a bad moment during the last training session. Kika was tail-walking: she was half out of the water, propelling herself backwards with her body upright. Jane made her repeat the tail-walk several times, and suddenly found there were no fish left for rewarding her. Daniel saw her frowning at the empty bucket, but he was saved by Pacho, who drenched Jane with a belly-flop at just the right moment.

Jane was still puzzled at the end of training. 'It's odd; if I didn't know better, I'd think somebody else had been working with her.'

Vicky giggled and avoided looking at Daniel. 'Well, I play catch with her, chasing leaves and things.'

'No, no.' Jane shook her head. 'It's almost as though I'm too slow for her, and she wants to go on to other things. Then sometimes she's very lazy, and won't jump as high as usual. I get the feeling I'm not stimulating her enough. Maybe she needs an audience to help push her along ... Look, there's that greedy pelican, back for more fish.'

The brown pelican landed on a post near the cooler and watched them with its head on one side. It had first appeared on the pier with a damaged wing, unable to fish for itself. They had fed it until the wing mended, and the bird still returned occasionally for a free handout. Daniel offered a fish, which the pelican dropped into its pouch and gulped down. It took off, wings spreading six feet across, and flew low over the brilliant blue sea, ready to swoop on any silvery flash.

'What are you two hoping to catch tonight?' said Jane to Vicky and Daniel. 'Oh, that reminds me, I must go and see if I can find an iron. I think that navy Captain might expect a woman to put on a dress for his party.'

Vicky waited until her mother was out of hearing. 'What are we hoping to catch? Oh, just some gold and silver and emeralds! Isn't it lucky she's going to that party? There won't be anyone to see us off.'

'There'll still be people around. We should go at dusk, when they're in the kitchen waiting for supper,' said Daniel. 'We'll start off from the dock, and go round the back of the island, then paddle up to the pier. I'll bring the fish for Kika, and my torch. I've got my fishing spear too – it's pretty strong.'

On her way back to the cabin, Vicky thought about the things she should take. She found her mother studying her reflection in the small mirror – she could only see part of herself at a time. She was wearing a close-fitting white dress to show off her tan. Smoothing it over her stomach, she said, 'I'm sure I've put on weight here – too much fried fish.'

'How will you climb on to the patrol ship in that?' asked Vicky.

It was a problem which hadn't occurred to Jane. 'I'll just have to hoick it up, as ladylike as I can. I haven't got anything else.'

Vicky pulled out her blue canvas bag and stuffed a towel and long-sleeved cotton shirt into it. She added her knife, a pen-light, the ten peso coins, the tin lid, the washers (Jane was too concerned with her eye make-up to be curious about what Vicky was packing), a toy compass which might be useful if it clouded over, and her gold chain. She'd also managed to wangle some egg sandwiches and oranges from the cook, as they'd be missing supper.

'How do I look?' asked Jane.

'Great,' said Vicky, glancing at her. 'Why didn't I get your blue eyes? Everyone's nuts about blue eyes in Colombia.'

'Jane! Are you coming?' It was Antonio outside. 'Wow!'

'Just because you never see me dressed up. . . . Vicky, you're not to stay out too late – and wear something over your bathing suit.' Vicky nodded, hopping from one foot to the other, and practically pushing her mother down the path. 'You seem very excited about your fishing! Have fun.'

It was just getting dark, with a strange orange-grey light overhead; the moon was half full, and already high in the sky. Vicky listened for Antonio's engine to fade, then picked up her bag and ran to the dock. Daniel was in the boat, checking the fuel, the painter and the paddle. He had brought some fishing gear too.

'I'll go and make sure there's no one around the aquarium.' Vicky walked through the restaurant. She could hear some singing and laughter in the kitchen, and the pier was deserted.

They did a long slow loop around the island, then Daniel cut the engine and started paddling. It was very calm. He slid the big canoe in under the pier and told Vicky to wait while he freed the bottom of the fence. Kika bobbed up the other side of the wire. After three dives, Daniel swam back to the boat, saying he'd pulled the mesh as far open as possible.

Vicky put on her mask and flippers, and slipped into the water with some fish in her hand. She waved the fish at Kika through the fence and dived down to the hole. She could see surprisingly well. Phosphorescent sparks seemed to fly from her fingers as she swam through the water. Kika was looking at her through the hole and Vicky tried to tempt her with a fish. Then she had to go up for air.

'Please, please Kika,' she prayed, willing Kika to come out. She swam half through the hole, showing the dolphin there was no danger. This time Kika came forward until her snout was outside. But she twisted abruptly and swam back into the pen. Vicky waited on the surface for her to return. She could hear an outboard in the distance, and imagined her mother coming back early to find Kika gone. Then she saw Kika's shadow and dived for the hole again. Kika shot through before Vicky could even offer her a fish. Hurriedly, she yanked the mesh down.

'She's out, start paddling – and throw me the painter,' called Vicky. She pulled herself along the rope until she was just behind the stern. They heard a loud puff to the left – Kika was still with them.

Vicky was suddenly terrified of the dark sea. She began to imagine all the creatures she couldn't see, and drew her knees tight against her chest. Daniel was paddling strongly; soon they were clear of the island reef. Vicky couldn't bear to stay in the water any longer.

'I'll get in; let's try the motor.' Daniel helped her aboard. She was shaking. 'It's cold,' she said, although she knew it wasn't. 'Wait a moment, I'll see if Kika wants to eat, otherwise she might go off chasing fish.' She slapped the water, and Kika snatched the fish from her hand.

Daniel started the motor, hoping the noise wouldn't drive Kika away. They went slowly, Vicky crouched in the bow, calling her constantly. After a few minutes Kika porpoised ahead of them.

'Hurray!' yelled Vicky.

Daniel grinned in relief, looked up at the stars and picked out Orion. He stood in the stern, one hand on the outboard, confident that he could find the Bell Reef by instinct, especially on such a still, bright night.

10 Thursday night: the disk

Kika didn't wander far from the boat; it was as though she preferred to stay close to something familiar. Vicky and Daniel shouted encouragement; Vicky had begun to enjoy herself – it was a magnificent night. Everything was going so well, she was convinced they'd be riding back ankle-deep in treasure.

Daniel reckoned it would take nearly an hour to the reef at the speed they were doing; he was anxious not to tire Kika. There were lights on the far side of the government island: fishermen or smugglers, he thought. A large fish jumped fifty yards away from the boat, sending up a shower of sparkling spray. Kika showed no interest. Could she sense they had something specific to do? Some islanders believed dolphins were exceptional creatures, and that it was unlucky to harm them.

When she thought they were nearing the reef, Vicky moved to the prow of the canoe and kept her eyes fixed on the water just ahead. She wasn't sure whether she would be able to distinguish the pale turquoise of the shallower sea. Daniel shone his new torch straight down

by the side of the boat, and the beam suddenly caught a mass of brilliantly coloured fish. He stopped the motor; they drifted on a little, trying to see which part of the reef they were on. Vicky held a fish out for Kika, and she took it immediately, despite the shoals of live fish around her.

Daniel announced they were too far along, and paddled back, helped by a slight current. He concentrated on the noise of the paddle cutting into the water and the sound of Kika's breathing to blot out the gloomy stillness of the ocean. He often went fishing at night in the islands, but now his grandfather's warnings whirred round in his head, making him uneasy.

'One of us will have to dive down to look for the place. I . . . I'm afraid of sharks.' Vicky hated sounding cowardly. She simply couldn't force herself into the water again.

'Oh, you don't have to worry about sharks,' said Daniel, adding to himself, it's the things without flesh and fins and teeth you should be afraid of. He checked that they were near the end of the reef, adjusted his mask and slipped the torch handle over his wrist: he didn't want the torch to join his knife on the reef. The water felt unusually clammy. Daniel was overcome by sickening thoughts of human bones picked clean by fish, and reached for the side of the canoe.

'Why are you waiting?' Vicky's voice pushed for action.

A couple of deep breaths, and he was kicking into a forest of dazzling richness, lit up by the narrow beam of his torch. Corals stretched out their tentacles to catch food, forming beautiful coloured haloes. The fish didn't seem to mind the light – some were obviously dopey with sleep. Odd shapes and shadows flitted around him. A small octopus danced away into the darkness. It all looked so different at night. He searched for a glint of gold along the edge of the reef, but the only glints he could see were the tiny red eyes of darting shrimp. Kika suddenly whirled by, startling him.

'I don't know if I can find the gold disk; it might have been covered by sand, anyway,' he said to Vicky. She was impatient to set Kika to work before she got bored and swam off in search of other dolphins. Daniel climbed back into the boat.

With a fish in one hand and the biscuit tin lid in the other, Vicky leant over the edge to attract Kika's attention. It was only a moment before Kika popped up, her mouth already open.

'Turn the torch on me,' said Vicky to Daniel. Then she held the lid out – it shone well in the torch's light – and signalled down to the sea-bed. Kika dived, and stayed under for what seemed an age.

'She won't get anything,' said Daniel pessimistically. 'We must be mad.'

He was right. Kika jumped a few yards away, and came to the canoe. Vicky offered her a fish even though she knew it was unforgivable to break the reward system. They tried again with no result. Kika swam round and round the canoe in frustration, then disappeared. She was behaving strangely, but Vicky couldn't tell whether it was the effect of being out in the open sea, or the atmosphere of the reef itself.

'It's too difficult – it's deep and there's all that stuff on the bottom. And we aren't even sure if we're in the right place,' said Vicky. She felt Kika's failure was her fault. 'I guess we should be glad she's taking any notice of us at all. I don't suppose she could care an atom what there is down there. I'll try an iron washer next.'

Daniel shone the torch downwards; they were already some way off the reef. He paddled back half-heartedly.

Kika announced her return with a lot of high-pitched squeaking. Vicky showed her the washer, and she dived with a flourish of her flukes.

'She'll probably bring us a crab so we stop bothering her,' said Vicky. She groaned when

Kika came up: there was a large chunk of coral wedged between her teeth. Vicky almost dropped it. 'It's terribly heavy,' she complained as she threw it in the boat, 'maybe there's some old iron or something inside. What shall we do? Go on and on?'

For different reasons, neither of them wanted to get into the water to check the position. Kika had now eaten a lot of fish, and it would become harder and harder to persuade her to obey their commands. The whole trip was beginning to seem more like a senseless risk than a glorious adventure. To add to their worries Kika had stopped answering their signals.

'We'll just have to wait until she turns up. I have a coin here, in case. We might as well have something to eat.' Vicky gave Daniel a sandwich and an orange. They sat under the stars, small waves lapping against the side of the canoe, which rose and fell gently in the swell. Vicky, ever-hopeful, was convinced Kika would return, but the waiting made Daniel uncomfortable. The feeling that they shouldn't be there, that they were trespassing, stopped him from throwing out a fishing-line. But there was nothing obviously threatening – it was warm, and light enough to see that there were no distant squalls to whip up the sea.

Vicky munched through a sandwich, dropping crumbs which disappeared instantly, snatched by small fish. She started peeling an orange with her pen-knife. A sudden swish and a loud puff told them Kika was back. Quickly, Vicky grabbed the coin and held it out to Kika, pointing to the sea-bed with the pen-knife in her other hand. They were no longer expecting any spectacular results, but Vicky scrabbled around in the canoe for a fish to give Kika when she re-surfaced.

'She's got something!' shouted Daniel. 'She's got my knife ... and there's something else hanging down too!'

Vicky eased Daniel's knife out of Kika's mouth; it was still wound up in the fishing-line they had used. She stood up and pulled the line clear of the water. 'It's the disk, the gold disk! It's jammed on to the fishing hook ... look!' Kika sensed the excitement and bobbed up again; Vicky stroked her head, babbling congratulations.

Daniel examined the disk in the light of his torch. It was about four inches across, and not as heavy as he'd imagined. There was a raised pattern all around the edge, and two holes on opposite sides. The hook had caught in one of them. He'd originally said the design might be a cross – in fact, it was a man who looked as if he was doing a knee-bend; a long bar rested across his shoulders. The face was a triangle, and the eyes, nose, and mouth showed as faint bumps in the gold surface. They stared at it, fascinated.

'I think it may be very old – I mean from before the Spaniards,' said Daniel.

'D'you realise why she found it?'

Daniel shook his head. 'No.' In the dark, he hadn't seen what Vicky had been holding.

'It's fantastic – I had my knife in my hand because I was peeling the orange. Kika must have thought I was telling her to look for a knife; she can't even have seen the coin!'

Daniel pursed his lips, astonished at Vicky's luck.

'Let's try the coin once more, you never know,' said Vicky ruffling the water to call Kika.

Then it happened – what Daniel had been dreading all the evening: a sudden ringing from the depths, eerier and more frightening than ever. It was nothing like as loud as it had been underwater, but it was infinitely more unearthly in the still moonlight. Neither of them spoke. They just sat. Daniel thought he could hear distant voices, then realised that Vicky was whispering.

'Kika's gone. If she was anywhere near that, she won't come back here tonight.' Vicky tried to imagine how a dolphin, with such sensitive hearing, would behave in the open sea.

Daniel was reluctant to start the outboard – he wasn't sure why: they'd never stayed on the reef after hearing the clanging, and he felt as though something else was about to happen. The haunting sound seemed to ring over and over again in his head.

'Come on,' insisted Vicky, 'we must start going back; she'll probably join us on the way. Don't go too fast.'

'Okay.' He pulled the cord, and the outboard sputtered. He revved up and shifted into forward gear. The boat leapt forward, then jerked to a halt, the motor roaring. Daniel was knocked on to his knees. Vicky fell hard against the planking.

'What's wrong?' she asked, shaken.

'I don't know. Something's holding us here. The painter's in the boat, isn't it?' He flashed his torch at the bow. 'Yes.' He cut the motor and bent over the stern. 'Come and look,' he said, shining the torch down into the water. A thick rope was tangled round the propeller shaft. It stretched tautly down towards the ocean floor.

'Where . . . how . . . ' began Vicky.

'Have you forgotten – the rope we saw the other day? It's got us.' Daniel slumped down in the boat. 'It's got us.'

'But it can't . . . it's only a rope,' said Vicky practically. 'We'll unwind it, or cut it. Where's your knife?'

For once, Daniel was glad of her bossiness. It jolted him back to the real world. He looked over the stern again, and saw the rope had loosened. The last thing he wanted to do was dive into the sea.

'Can you hold on to my ankles? I'm going to lean right over the edge.' He put his arms into the water and felt the shaft, and the rope looped around it. Working the loops down and over the propeller, he freed them in a few seconds. This time the canoe surged forward when he started up.

After ten minutes with the motor going flat out, the lights on the government island winked low on the horizon. Daniel kept far out and slackened speed. They continued homewards slowly, shouting and smacking the water with the paddle. Twice they heard splashes which turned out to be fish. There was no sign of Kika – not a puff, not a squeak, not a leap. Vicky was hopeful; Daniel was thinking that Kika was worth much more than a golden disk. He remembered his grandfather's words about greed. At one point he shut the motor off and they drifted for a while, calling out into the darkness.

'How could we have done it? How could

I have thought it would work?' said Daniel miserably.

'Well, I did too,' said Vicky firmly. 'And I still do. Where would Kika go if she was scared out of her wits? Of course, back to the pen! Maybe she's there . . . '

Daniel was already up on his feet and starting the engine.

Vicky was so convincing that they imagined Kika porpoising to and fro outside the dolphin pen.

This cheered them up for the last stretch, and Daniel considered what they should do with the disk: sell it and share the profit? Keep it? Let a diver in on the secret and see whether there was any more gold down there? He shuddered at the idea of going back to the reef – yet it didn't seem quite as impossible as it had half an hour ago.

His dreams collapsed when he saw the fence – Kika wasn't there. Even Vicky wasn't so optimistic now, but she voted against a sea search; if Kika wanted to come she would, especially when she got hungry, said Vicky more sensibly than she really felt. Tired and deflated, they motored round to the dock. Antonio's boat wasn't back yet – it must be a good party. Vicky scooped all the bits and pieces from the bottom of the canoe into her canvas bag and went back to the cabin. She chucked the bag untidily in a corner and sat on the bed. Suddenly all her confidence in Kika's return dissolved. She burst into tears, then crawled into bed and fell asleep, exhausted.

Daniel wandered back to the pier. He was too depressed to go home; the only thing that mattered was finding Kika. He nearly threw the gold disk into the water; if he returned it to the sea perhaps Kika would reappear? But it seemed a pointless, melodramatic thing to do. He settled down on the end of the pier to keep watch. At least Pacho and Molly were safely inside. His head fell forward on to his chest as he dozed.

11 Friday morning: the navy steps in

Vicky was still half asleep – she didn't want to face her mother or the day, even though it was uncomfortably hot in bed. Jane put on shorts and a shirt, and tried to find some sandals to wear. As she pushed aside Vicky's canvas bag, two oranges and a mess of coral and rock tipped out with a heavy clunk.

'I know you're awake,' she said to Vicky. 'I've got some extraordinary news! But I'm desperate for coffee so you'll have to drag yourself along to the restaurant.' The door closed behind her.

Horrified, Vicky sat up in bed. Had her mother been out to the dolphins the night before, and seen Kika was missing? No, it couldn't be that – she'd sounded excited. Vicky pulled on her red bathing suit, splashed some water over her face, and ran along the path.

'That was quick,' Jane grinned. Daniel was with her, looking surprisingly unconcerned.

'Come on, Mum, don't be unfair, tell us,' begged Vicky.

'Well, you know our friend Ray Macdonald? The navy arrested him last night.'

'What?' said Vicky and Daniel together.

'Yes, really. He had set up camp on the government island, so they got him for trespassing. Of course, everyone knows he was looking for treasure: he had a metal detector, and some machine like a giant underwater vacuum cleaner for moving sand, as well as lots of diving equipment. They say he hadn't really got going yet.'

'But, where . . . did you go too?' asked Vicky enviously.

'Oh, no. Antonio says they planned the party especially. Most of the people who have houses on the islands were invited, and everyone knew. The Captain arranged it so Macdonald would think the patrol ship was far too busy with the party to bother about him. Apparently there were lights at his camp, and no look-out or anything. The Lieutenant took some sailors in a small boat – one of those inflatable rafts – and they went to the bay this side of the island, then walked through. They were back with Macdonald and two other gringos before we left. It caused quite a stir.'

'Do they know where he was exploring?' asked Daniel, who had managed to understand most of the story, with a little translation help from Vicky.

'No, I don't think so. Nobody mentioned any maps or charts; but the Captain's very reserved about that sort of thing. It's a bit difficult to accuse someone of *planning* a treasure hunt. The Captain said they'd probably find an excuse to expel Macdonald from Colombia – after all, trespassing isn't a very serious crime.'

Vicky looked across at Daniel. 'Mum, do you know if treasure hunting is actually against the law?'

Jane thought about it. 'Antonio could tell you more than I can. I don't suppose looking for treasure is illegal, but most countries have laws covering the salvage of treasure. I mean, if you took something, that would probably be illegal. Why such interest?' She glanced at her watch. 'We should be out with the dolphins.'

Daniel went ahead to get the fish ready. Vicky hung back, delaying as long as possible. Surely Daniel would have let her know if Kika was back.

Jane turned as they went through the aquarium. 'Come on, you're very quiet this morning, you haven't said a word about your fishing trip – you were dead to the world when I came in . . . Why, what is it?' Vicky's face lit up like a smiling sun, and she skipped round her mother.

'I just saw Kika jump, that's all,' she said happily. 'There she goes again!'

'What's so special about Kika jumping? You are in a funny mood today,' said Jane. 'Daniel's all smiles too. You must have had a good time.'

Kika was in very high spirits, and thoroughly disobedient. Jane gave up halfway through the training session, turning her attention to Pacho and Molly.

'I don't know what's got into Kika – let's hope she settles down later,' said Jane. Vicky was having trouble containing her giggles, and Daniel pretended not to notice. 'Or what's got into you two for that matter. Vicky, I'm going to arrange for a bed to be made up in the cabin loft – you'll be sleeping there if Dad comes out today, right?'

As soon as Jane had gone, Vicky burst out: 'You knew Kika was back, didn't you? And you didn't say anything!'

Daniel nodded. 'It was worth it, just to see your face.' And he told Vicky what had happened early that morning: the first rays of the sun woke him. He was cramped and muzzy after a night on the wooden slats, and had that horrible leaden feeling that everything was wrong. He heard a dolphin breathe just below him, near the pier. Wait a minute, he thought, a dolphin near the pier? Pacho and

114

Molly never came over this side of the pen. He leapt up. Kika! There she was, surveying the pier from her 'look-out' position. Daniel was so delighted he dived straight into the sea. A string of squeaks and whistles greeted him underwater. He lifted the wire mesh; Kika needed no encouragement to go through the fence into the pen. She swam over to Pacho and Molly, and the three of them wheeled around, stroking one another with their flippers. Daniel was tempted to go and wake Vicky, but he decided to have a coffee, and wait for her to appear.

'Isn't that something about Macdonald?' said Daniel.

'Isn't it? Where's the gold disk?' asked Vicky.

'Here, in the box by the cooler.' They got it out for another look.

'You heard what Mum said, we could be arrested for taking it. What shall we do?'

'Oh, I don't think—'

Daniel was interrupted by a shout from Jane. 'Vicky, come to the cabin at once – and you too, Daniel.' She sounded upset.

They found her bending over Vicky's canvas bag, picking at bits of coral.

'What's all this stuff here? Where did you get it?' She held out a handful of coral and shells – and dull grey metal.

Daniel scrabbled on the floor and found

116

more. They gazed at it in amazement. The rock discovered by Kika had broken up as a result of being dropped on the cement floor. Encrusted in the coral was a cluster of irregular, chunky coins.

'They're old silver coins,' said Jane. 'Pieces of eight.'

'That's why it was so heavy. But how did Kika . . . ' began Vicky, and stopped and bit her lip.

Jane stared at her. 'I think I'd better hear all about this,' she said.

It took Vicky a long time to tell the whole story, from the noise of the bell to the gold disk and the part played by Kika. Daniel interrupted a couple of times to make sure she included all the details. Jane just listened, astonished that so much could have been going on without her realising. She was horrified by their irresponsibility in freeing Kika, yet fascinated to hear how she had behaved. They showed her the gold disk.

'I'm sure Daniel's right – it must be pre-Columbian. I've seen work like it in the gold museum in Bogotá. Now,' she continued briskly, 'we have to decide what to do next. We'll talk about Kika later. When I think of all the things that could have happened to her – I can't believe you two could be so stupid.' She looked disappointed rather than angry.

'Anyway, if there's really an old wreck on the Bell Reef – and the coins certainly suggest there may be – we should tell Captain Mendoza before you get into any more trouble. Let's ask Antonio what he thinks.'

Antonio was furious when he heard how they had taken Kika out to the reef. So much so that Daniel was afraid he would be sacked on the spot. But Antonio wanted to leave straightaway to find the naval patrol boat and hand over the coins and the disk.

They saw the grey boat – a large ocean-going tug – heading towards the government island, and caught up as it was anchoring. The Captain, impressive in his uniform, asked if they'd arrived to see the fun. He was about to load the equipment from Macdonald's camp. Macdonald himself had already been sent to Cartagena in his own boat, with the Lieutenant in charge. They boarded, and everyone sat down at a table in a long, low-ceilinged room. Vicky and Daniel, both very subdued, gave the Captain a shortened version of their trips to the Bell Reef. He didn't say much, and called the archaeologist to look at their finds.

'That gold disk probably comes from the Tairona culture – the figures often represented the sun, and had a religious meaning. Have you been to the Sierra Nevada mountains?' Vicky and Daniel both said no. 'Well, the

Tairona lived in the mountains, further up the Colombian coast. They were one of the most advanced groups here at the time of the Spanish conquest.

'Now, let's see the coins; they'll have to be cleaned up carefully. The ones on the outside are badly corroded, but these in the middle may tell us something.' He worked one of the coins loose and pulled it free of the cluster. It was shaped like a roughly-made hexagon, with six edges of different lengths. One side was rubbed very smooth; the other showed two pillars topped by a crown, and there was lettering across the centre.

'This is excellent,' said the archaeologist. 'Look, there's the date, quite clear.' He pointed out a figure – 95 – at the bottom between the pillars. 'That would be 1695. The eight on the top under the crown gives its value – eight reales; that's why they were called pieces of eight. Then this P on the left means it was minted in Potosí, in the mountains of Bolivia. Potosí was the world's biggest silver mine, and highlanders slaved away there to produce coins for the Spanish empire. Do you know anything more about this reef?' he asked.

Vicky explained about the story she'd started to read in the library. She wasn't sure whether an archaeologist would think a book of tales and traditions was a silly place to look for information. But he was interested, and wanted any snippets she could remember. He said the stern governor in the story might be Diaz Pimienta, who ruled Cartagena in the early 1700s – it fitted in with the date of the coin, too.

'That would make it about the same time as the *San José* – interesting,' said the Captain.

Then Daniel told them about his grandfather's warning.

'And you went back at night in spite of all that?' said the archaeologist. 'Well, I think it was very enterprising of you.'

Captain Mendoza and Antonio seemed irritated by his approval of such immature behaviour. But Jane suddenly realised that she hadn't considered the venture from that point of view. It was true, they'd been most imaginative and even – she had to admit it – rather sensible in the way they'd planned the whole thing.

'Why didn't you tell someone when you first saw the gold?' asked the Captain.

'We weren't sure . . . ' mumbled Vicky.

Jane helped her out: 'Captain, would you have taken it seriously if two kids said they thought they saw a gold disk at the bottom of a reef? Vicky, Daniel, why don't you go out on deck for a moment, and we'll have a conference.'

They picked their way past coils of rope to the stern.

'You're not too fed up that I let it out?' asked Vicky.

'No . . . when she found the coins, what else could we have done?' said Daniel despondently. 'It's all right for you. I'm sure I'll lose my job. Antonio's very angry about Kika. He thinks he can't trust me any more.'

Vicky hadn't given Daniel's job a thought. She felt ashamed, but couldn't think of anything hopeful or comforting to say.

They leaned over the rail and watched the long-handled metal detector being lifted on to the boat. It was followed by air tanks, bulging waterproof sacks, tangled ropes and several large plastic containers.

Jane came up behind them. 'What a gloomy pair. You're not going to the dungeons, you know; in fact, we're so close to the Bell Reef that the Captain's decided to take a look. He's a professional diver and he's going to fit Antonio out too. And Daniel, don't worry too much, I think I can talk Antonio round.' He nodded gratefully. 'We're going in Antonio's boat; come on, Daniel, you're in charge.'

They climbed awkwardly down the rope ladder and pushed off. Vicky had recovered her bounce, and Daniel looked a lot happier. He went slower than normal, keeping level with

121

the Captain, Antonio, and the archaeologist in the inflatable raft. Daniel found the end of the reef easily, but there wasn't much he and Vicky could do without masks. The boat wallowed in the swell as they waited for the others to test their tanks and respirators.

'Here, look after our raft,' shouted the Captain, throwing his painter over.

The water wasn't very clear, but they could see the divers' shapes from above. Vicky slopped sea-water on her head to cool down. The high, thin cloud produced a harsh white light that seemed to burn more fiercely than the sun. It was fifteen minutes before the three men surfaced. Vicky and Daniel waited impatiently for them to board the raft and pull alongside.

'An extraordinarily rich reef,' said the Captain. 'I haven't seen coral growth like that for a long time.'

'But . . . what about the wreck?' said Vicky.

The archaeologist answered her. 'There must have been a big storm recently, shifting the sand behind the reef.' Daniel nodded, remembering how the storm had altered the beach near his house. 'I saw some half-buried timber about fifty yards out – could well be remnants of an old keel. There may be a lot more hidden down there, but we have to go about it scientifically.'

Captain Mendoza laughed for the first time

122

that day. 'You're making it sound very dull to these two adventurers. It's true a slave ship wouldn't carry a treasure like the *San José*'s. But any ship of that age is exciting. It may be just old timbers and dinner plates,' Vicky looked dismayed, 'or a cache of emeralds; and anyway, that disk can't be the only piece of gold.'

The archaeologist nodded. 'By the way, I can see why it's called the Bell Reef: there's an enormous old diving bell on its side at the foot of the reef. Somebody must have tried to salvage the ship soon after it sank.'

'A bell . . . on its side?' questioned Daniel, puzzled. He asked if he could borrow a mask and flippers, then dived where the archaeologist showed him. The reef was utterly changed by day, with none of the spookiness of the night before.

'Vicky, you must come and have a look,' said Daniel when he surfaced.

She tightened the Captain's mask on, and went down with him.

The sea was cloudy, but she saw a shadowy bell-shape tipped over on the sand. It could have been a huge church bell, big enough to allow two or three people to stand upright under it. The outside was camouflaged by coral growth, the inside seemed to be smooth metal. They went up to breathe together.

123

'Did you see the rope?' asked Daniel. She shook her head, and he told her to follow him down. Attached to the top of the bell, draped over rocky outcrops, was the thick rope which had ensnared the propellor.

'The bell – it wasn't like that the other day,' said Daniel when they were back in the boat. 'I think I must have seen it, but it looked more like a mound of coral. I wouldn't have noticed, except for the rope dangling in the water.'

'Well, if you ask me the bell's fallen over on its side very recently – the inside's so clean,' said Antonio. 'And that rope is new ... I wonder whether it was anything to do with Macdonald. You found some ropes and marker buoys among his stuff, didn't you?'

The Captain nodded. 'You could be right. Now we'll have some well-informed questions to put to him. He hasn't told us a thing; he kept saying he thought he'd been jinxed.'

Daniel had been thinking about the bell. 'Last night, when the rope caught round the propellor, we may have pulled the bell over.' He described what had happened, and everyone agreed it was the most likely explanation.

Neither Vicky nor Daniel had said much about the clanging noise – they'd left out a lot of details after first telling the story to Jane. And neither of them wanted to raise it with the business-like Captain. Yet they were both

124

disturbed by the sight of the empty bell. What had caused the ringing? Daniel decided it was time to hear what his grandfather knew about Bell Reef. It would only be fair to include Vicky too. Now that they knew so much, surely he would fill in the gaps.

They waved goodbye and headed back to the island with Antonio at the wheel. Nobody had said anything about the value of the disk and coins, or whether Vicky and Daniel could hope for a share.

12 Friday afternoon: the bell

It had been a hectic morning, and they went straight to the restaurant for a late lunch. Just as she was starting on her crab salad, Jane remembered that the dolphins had missed the second training session, and the food that went with it.

'For once they can wait,' she said. 'Kika probably ate all sorts of titbits out in the ocean. No wonder she was so impossible this morning.'

'Mum, now you know Kika would come back to the pen, can't you leave her free?' The morning had restored Vicky's self-confidence, and she was sure her mother's anger had evaporated.

Jane looked at Antonio. 'Well?'

He had simmered down too. In fact he was wondering how Kika's new skill could be turned into an interesting addition to the show.

'I haven't told you two what I think of you yet – and it may be better if I don't. But this is a serious warning: any more fooling like that, and you'll be off this island for good.' He looked sternly from one to the other. Daniel was tremendously relieved – he hadn't been fired. 'As to Kika, it's not so simple. If we have part of the fence open, other things can enter the pen: remember the spotted ray; think of a shark: it might not be dangerous to a full-grown dolphin in the open sea, but could turn very nasty in a small space.'

Antonio tipped his cap on to the back of his head, and tapped the table thoughtfully. 'If we taught Kika to jump the fence, she could easily injure herself. I can imagine one possible solution: suppose we make a gate in the fence, and let her out when there's someone with her. Come to think of it, the visitors would probably love that, and there's no reason why we shouldn't try it with Pacho and Molly too.'

Jane nodded in agreement: 'Speaking of dolphins, it's time we fed them.'

Daniel leapt up and ran off to the storeroom with Vicky not far behind.

'It's great that you haven't lost your job. And . . . ' Vicky stumbled. 'If . . . if we get something for the gold disk, maybe we could buy an outboard motor for your canoe?'

Daniel was loading the wheelbarrow. He went on packing in the small pearlfish while he thought about what she'd said. An outboard! He grinned. 'You're always so optimistic. I bet we never hear anything more about that disk.'

Kika was hungry again, which made her very willing. She seemed to jump effortlessly, and sliced into the water cleanly. Jane tried the pick-up using Vicky's signal, and Kika brought her the whistle without any hesitation. To make it more difficult, Jane threw in a coin, an iron washer and a stone, close together. She showed Kika another coin; they saw Kika swim from one object to the other, clicking furiously, then take the coin in her mouth.

'I'm just a bit worried that she might swallow one of these things,' said Jane, who was very impressed. 'I'll have to work out a safe routine. It's a good way of teaching people how dolphins use their echo system. We could try blindfolding Kika too: that would make it even more dramatic. You know, I'm still amazed that she followed your orders out in the ocean. Normally, she's very fussy about where I stand – she'll only go through the hoop if I hold it out on this end of the platform.'

After training Daniel wired the fence up while Antonio and Jane discussed the possibility of a trap-door in the mesh. Sensing that all had been forgiven, Daniel asked if he could take Vicky over to meet his grandfather.

'Come back before dark,' said Jane. 'Dad's due tonight.'

As they were getting into Daniel's canoe

Luis appeared with a large carrier bag full of groceries.

'Your father left this for you. He said he didn't get the shorts because there wasn't enough money – that you would understand.'

Daniel did understand. His father had run out of money and had used Daniel's pesos to pay for his mother's shopping. That was the last time he asked his father to bring anything, thought Daniel resentfully.

The small canoe was low in the water, and the afternoon breeze lifted enough spray to soak them. Daniel's house – a weathered, thatched hut – was sheltered by a spit of land and some mangroves. Vicky, barefoot, picked her way carefully over the broken coral beach, exclaiming 'Ouch!' every few seconds. Two small girls came running out, one of them carrying a baby.

'It's the gringa, the foreign girl!' shouted the bigger girl excitedly. Daniel's mother, a small, slightly anxious-looking woman, welcomed Vicky with a smile and Daniel with a frown.

'You should have told me. The house is such a mess.' She ticked Daniel off and disappeared inside with the shopping.

They went round to the far side of the house, where Daniel's grandfather was bent over an old circular fishing-net. Hidden by a straw hat, he went on checking the lead weights around the edge of the net.

'You might like to use this for casting. I'd forgotten it was up among the thatch.' He looked up. 'So this is the gringa, is it? And you two have been nosing around where you had no business.' He chuckled suddenly, as if he realised he'd made Vicky feel uncomfortable. 'So now you've come to ask the old man to explain it all for you.'

They said yes, and sat on the ground by him.

He leaned back, and took his hat off. 'Once I told the story to a man who was collecting tales and traditions from these parts. He said he would write them in a book. I thought I was done for at the time, but fate decided I should live a little longer.'

'I saw the story,' said Vicky, 'but I didn't have time to read much of it.'

'So he really did put it in a book, did he?' Daniel's grandfather seemed pleased. He raised his voice: 'You women in there, aren't you going to bring us some refreshment?'

'I'm making some lemonade,' called Daniel's mother.

'Well . . . let's see.' He began in almost exactly the same words as those Vicky had read in the library. He told how the French smuggler had been paid for 150 slaves in silver and gold, and had run into a storm soon after leaving for Portobelo with 250 slaves still on board.

'The rudder was torn away in the heavy seas, and the ship was careering over the Treasure Banks; those dangerous shoals have sunk many ships, but this one had a different destiny. The slaves were packed below decks, cursing and chanting in the darkness, and calling on their African gods.

'Deep in a trough, between two waves higher than the tallest palm trees, the ship hit a reef. The timbers were battered and shredded by rocky coral; a trailing anchor caught, holding the ship against the jagged reef. She sank where she had struck; every slave drowned that night, for all 250 of them were chained one to another.

'But the Frenchman and two or three of his crew survived. They were rescued by island fishermen the next day. The Frenchman could think of nothing but the ship and cargo he had lost. Years later, when he had enough money to try salvaging the wreck, he returned to the reef. He promised some islanders a share of whatever they could recover. The islanders could dive deep, but they could not remain below long enough to work on the wreck. So the Frenchman brought a giant bronze bell to the reef. It was lowered on a rope and hung a few yards above the sea-floor. The divers could rest and breathe the air trapped inside it. They did not take to the bell, though; they said it made them feel dizzy and disorientated. Nor did they like disturbing the grave of so many souls.

'They found a few gold pieces: the slave dealer from Cartagena had paid with coins, and with other gold objects stolen from ancient tombs along the coast. The Frenchman said there was much more down there. He believed he was being cheated, and accused the divers of hiding away the treasure for themselves. He was determined to have a look. He dived down the side of the reef on a calm day. But he had weaker lungs than the islanders, and had barely reached the sea-bed when he swam into the bell for air.

'Nobody can be sure what happened next. Whatever the reason, most agree that the Frenchman was the victim of his own greed.'

Daniel's mother served them all lemonade. The old man drank his down without a pause. Vicky and Daniel, unmoving as statues, didn't touch theirs.

'The divers said they heard fearful swearing, and saw hundreds of black arms stretching up from the sand to seize the bell. Those in the boat up above said there was a tremendous drag on the bell – the pressure was so strong that the pulley snapped and the rope tore away; the

132

bell plunged to the bottom with the Frenchman inside it. Others, who were not there at the time, said the Frenchman had been murdered by the islanders.

'From that day, anyone who swims near the bell hears the warning. People believe the Frenchman is still hammering on the inside, trying to get out. They say that if the noise isn't enough to drive prying divers away, strange accidents happen.'

'But, Grandfather, if the bell fell over on its side, the Frenchman would be free and the clanging noise would stop, wouldn't it?' asked Daniel.

'That could be. I don't like the idea of the Frenchman's spirit roaming free, but perhaps it's time . . . and it seems right that a descendant of one of the divers should be the person to lift the spell, if that is what has happened.'

Daniel was satisfied. His grandfather was showing approval in his roundabout way.

Vicky was more direct: 'Do you mean Daniel is descended from one of those divers?'

'How else do you think I know the story?' grinned the old man. 'My grandfather told me, his father told him – and so on, until you get back to a diver who worked for the Frenchman.'

Vicky envied this long family tree, and looked at Daniel with interest. Embarrassed,

133

he got up, saying they must go. Vicky had been sitting cross-legged so long that her legs had gone to sleep and she couldn't walk; her agonised antics broke the serious mood and made Daniel's sisters giggle.

They paddled back to the aquarium in friendly silence. The sky was painted with pink and gold streaks, and the wind gusted strongly, helping them along.

Jane waved them over to the pier. 'You've missed some more excitement. The Captain sent someone over with a message. You're both to go to the naval base on Monday. Don't look so alarmed! He says it should be possible to register your claim to the wreck on the Bell Reef. Then if it's salvaged, you might get something. I wouldn't order your yacht too soon, though,' she warned as Vicky grabbed Daniel's arm and danced around him.

'We'll be rich! Kika, Kika,' shouted Vicky, 'do you hear that?'

'Kika, Kika!' echoed a voice from the other side of the pen.

'Who's that?' said Vicky.

'Kika, Kika!'

Daniel burst out laughing. 'It's the parrots!'

Kika drifted up to the surface on her back, pink tummy glistening and flippers waving.

'You all seem to be very merry.' None of them had seen Martin stroll out on to the pier.

134

'Dad! I didn't know you were here.' Vicky ran to hug him.

'I've just arrived. I could hear you cackling away with the parrots and the dolphins from the other side of the island. Anything happened this week?'